Brush with Death

Also by E.J. Stevens

Spirit Guide
Young Adult Series

She Smells the Dead
Spirit Storm
Legend of Witchtrot Road
Brush with Death

Ivy Granger
Urban Fantasy Series

Shadow Sight
Blood and Mistletoe: An Ivy Granger Novella

Dark Poetry Collections

From the Shadows
Shadows of Myth and Legend

Brush with Death

A Spirit Guide Novel

E.J. Stevens

Published by Sacred Oaks Press
Sacred Oaks, 221 Sacred Oaks Lane, Wells, Maine 04090

First Printing (trade paperback edition), October 2012

Stevens, E.J.
Brush with Death / E.J. Stevens

ISBN 9780984247561 (trade pbk.)

Printed in the United States of America

Chapter 1
Emma

I bit my lip to stifle a gasp. Simon was leaving another trail of kisses down my neck that made me tingle all over.

How could this be wrong, when it felt so right?

I am not the kind of girl who falls for the wrong guy. Really. My entire life has been a series of good choices. I have always done the responsible thing. So what was I doing here with an older guy?

Oh yes, the kisses. That had something to do with it, definitely.

I reached up to brush hair out of hungry eyes that promised a world of new pleasures. *Tease.* I slid my fingers along the line of scar tissue that crossed his handsome face, drawing a low rumble from his chest. Somehow that candle-wax smooth skin added to his amazing looks. I pressed myself against him, melting into Simon like I was made of wax too. With another growling rumble, he grasped my shoulders and gently pushed me away.

For someone who prided himself as a lady's man, he sure wasn't moving fast. Most guys my age are a raging river during spring rains and snow melt. They move fast and hard and are all over the damn place. Yuck. Simon is a river of honey, slow and sweet.

Not that I eat honey. I'm against bee oppression, but you get the idea.

Simon is a gentleman and I like that about him, but some days I wished he'd stop putting on the brakes. I wanted to continue our kissing, but I guess he could only take so much. Secretly, that made me feel crazy powerful.

So Simon was older and had a bad reputation. I knew all of that. I wasn't naïve. I had entered into this relationship with eyes wide open. In fact, I'd resisted my feelings for nearly a year.

What had changed? Hello, like, everything. My best friend was plagued by ghosts, her boyfriend was a werewolf, and I could talk to snakes. But the big change? I was about to graduate from high school. I'd already been accepted into the pre-med veterinary program at Tufts University, a state away. Even Cornell had sent a letter asking me to visit their campus. Everything was changing, fast. I would be leaving at summer's end. It was now or never.

Deep down, I knew that part of the reason I chose now was my recent brush with death. I had been in a car accident and was lucky to be alive. Surviving that accident had brought clarity to my feelings for Simon. When I woke up in the hospital, his was the face I longed to see.

I made my decision.

I decided to follow my heart. I chose us. I chose now. I didn't regret it for one second. Well, not really. Did I feel guilt, worry, and confusion? Hell yes, but I wasn't confused about my feelings for Simon. He made me inordinately happy. There was no denying that.

Our relationship, as Yuki would say, was made of awesome. Sure, Simon and I didn't agree on everything. That was part of the attraction. We could debate all of the things we disagreed on…intensely.

No, the thing I was having trouble with, the problem that made me hesitate each time I sank into Simon's arms, was the objection of my friends. Calvin and Yuki weren't the most normal couple in the world, so you'd think they'd be able to see outside the box of social norms. Unfortunately, they kept getting hung up on the details—Simon was older, he was a total bad boy, and a studly werewolf.

I guess they were used to me dating harmless human guys, like Gordy. I could understand that, to a point. If I continued dating normal high school guys, they wouldn't have to worry about me. But didn't their judging of my relationship make them hypocrites? Why couldn't they accept my choice?

Why couldn't my friends just get over it already?

Chapter 2
Simon

*A*s soon as I pushed Emma away, tension wracked her body like an unyielding electric current. I wanted to pull her back to me and kiss away the tears, which she remained unaware of, that rolled steadily down her flushed cheeks to glisten on the creamy pale skin of her neck.

But I could only provide a temporary distraction to Emma's troubled thoughts. I was not the cause of her frustration.

Well, we were adept at causing each other a high degree of *physical* frustration, but the issue eating away at Emma's happiness, like a hungry zombie gnoshing on brains, had another cause entirely.

That cause was the very reason that vampires and zombies filled my subconscious, and therefore my metaphors. Emma's best friend Yuki, an exasperating Goth girl who could sense ghosts through smells, didn't approve of our relationship.

Up until now, Yuki had refrained from the emo behavior typical of most Goth teens whom I'd encountered in the past. When I began training Yuki, I was impressed by her positive attitude and bull-headed stubbornness, though that stubbornness caused plenty of arguments between us. She had been through a lot in her short life and that was something I could relate to. I had even begun to entertain the notion that we could be friends.

But that was before I started dating Emma. Suddenly, Yuki acted like she'd been possessed by one of her smelly ghost mates, left to wail and moan and pout incessantly about the loss of her best friend to an old, nasty, roguish werewolf.

Where, I ask, is the fairness there?

Yuki herself is dating a werewolf, my alpha Calvin, so playing the *"you can't date a guy who shapeshifts into a wolf"* card was a pitiful attempt to derail our relationship. I can also assure you that I am not nasty. I maintain impeccable hygiene and grooming. And, if we are to cast stones, my wolf spirit smells like pine needles and puppy breath, unlike Calvin's spirit who reeks of wet dog.

As for the roguish bit, I've changed. I fully admit to a dark time in my life, before I met Emma. I did things that I am not proud of.

It is easy to be a scoundrel when you have nothing to live for.

Now I have an important role in my pack and a woman who I care for deeply. I am not the innocent man I was before the dark period of my life, before my first love Meredith died at the hands of a hunter and I cast my destiny to the wind…and the needle, but I hope that I am worthy of Emma's heart.

How will we ever know if we are truly destined for one another if Yuki continues to hold her friendship hostage? And Calvin is only making our situation worse by supporting Yuki's ridiculous behavior. I know deep within my shared soul that I can make Emma happy, if her friends would only give us a chance.

When I first met Emma and Yuki, I thought their bond was unbreakable…something seldom seen in humans. It angers me that my relationship with Emma should be the cause for that rare jewel of a friendship to shatter.

What the bloody hell are Calvin and Yuki thinking?

I balled my right fist and bit my knuckle hard enough to draw blood. I pulled my eyes from Emma's anguished, far-away gaze to look at the blood that pooled at the base of my thumb. Werewolves don't suck blood like pop-culture vampires, but in my world blood matters—just not in the way you think.

The blood of the Old Ones coursed through my veins, marking me as werewolf, as *other*, and aligning me to our pack. I obey my pack alpha, and have sworn to protect him with my very life, but I hadn't known then the pain that he would come to cause my new mate.

My bloodied hand would heal with a speed that was driven by my werewolf metabolism, but when would Emma's heart mend?

Chapter 3
Yuki

"What are we going to do?" I asked, throwing my hands in the air. "She's totally tossing her life away, right?"

"We don't know that," Cal said.

"Aren't you worried?" I asked.

"I'm worried about both of them," Cal said. "But mostly, I'm worried about you."

"Me?" I asked. "Have you been listening? Emma is dating Simon. *Simon.* Don't you find that, like, totally panic inducing?"

"Are you sure you're worried about Emma and not just missing your best friend?" Cal asked. "She's pretty tough and Simon isn't all bad. But you and Emma haven't spent this much time apart before. Maybe that's what you're actually worried about."

I sighed. Cal was right. I mean, sure, I was worried about my friend. Simon had this whole lady-killer persona and he was totally old, but I had to admit that more than anything, I was feeling hurt. It was like Emma had abandoned me for a shiny new toy. *More like a rusty old piece of junk.*

"When did you get so smart?" I asked.

"I was born this way," Cal said. "I just try to tone it down for the masses."

I poked him in the ribs and we both started laughing.

"Thanks," I said. I tilted my head up to look into Cal's blue eyes and felt a magnetic pull that beckoned me to lose myself utterly and completely in their azure depths.

"For what?" Cal said, raising one eyebrow.

"Making me laugh," I said. "I needed that."

There was something else I needed. *Kiss me.* All I had to do was think it and Cal's lips were on mine. That had been happening a lot lately. I'm not sure if it was a soul mate thing, but it was like Cal could read my mind. I just hoped he couldn't read every thought that passed through my head.

That would be embarrassing.

*****

Eventually we had to pull apart. School wouldn't wait for us. No matter how great the kisses, school office staff just wouldn't accept making out with Cal as a valid excuse for tardiness. I know this for a fact. Using kissing as a reason to be late for class? That stunt almost landed me in detention. I was going to try using it as an alternative for gym credit, but decided not to press my luck.

I flipped down the visor mirror and fixed my hair while Cal turned off his truck. Ghosts, school, death, and taxes; some things were just unavoidable.

Ugh, school. Things hadn't been so bad after I cleared my name and we helped turn in a gang of local drug dealers who were making meth in a lab off Witchtrot Road. For a while teachers treated us with more respect and students were nicer. That was actually kind of freaky at first. I'm used to being a total outsider that everyone at this school, except my small group of friends, ignores.

Well, *almost* everyone. Freshman year I was in the wrong place at the wrong time wearing my nonconformist Goth bling and caught the attention of the J-team. I've been on their radar ever since. It's not a fun place to be.

The J-team are bullies who enjoy tormenting other students, especially those who are smaller and weaker than them. The coups de grâce, the true nail in my coffin? The J-team hate anyone who dares to be different. They refuse to tolerate any student who shows a shred of individuality. Dress, act, talk, or (*gasp!*) think different and you are in for a world of hurt. Yeah, I do all of the above. I'm different and proud of it.

I might as well have a target painted on my fabulously Goth back.

The J-team, Jared Zempter and Jay Freeman, have gone out of their way to make every year that I attend Wakefield High a living hell. When their football teammate, Dylan Jacobs, died a few months ago, they blamed me. So. Not. Fair.

I definitely didn't have anything to do with Dylan's death, though I did help his ghost find peace, but the J-team rarely listen to reason. They are convinced that since I wear black clothing I must be a witch, so when Dylan died on a road with a legendary curse, they figured it was my fault. Personally, I think they just like tormenting me, but they managed to convince the entire football team of my guilt. That was not my finest moment. I almost peed myself. *But we'll keep that potential piece of gossip on the down-low.*

The J-team, with the help of their giganto jock friends, kidnapped me and stuck me in a school supply closet. Their brilliant plan? To convince me (*I think Jay was hoping for some torture, seriously the guy is creepy with a capital C*) to use my supposed witchy powers to bring Dylan back from the dead. I do have some connection with the dead, but that's my little secret. The J-team don't know that I can smell spirits of the dead. I've helped lots of ghosts find their way into the light. But resurrection? So not in my job description.

Fortunately for me, my dung beetle spirit guide clued me in on a way to contact Cal's wolf spirit and my friends came to the rescue. No black magic zombie jock raising here. That's a very good thing. Aside from the obvious downside of a brain munching football player, I'm also sure that if anyone in Wakefield ever managed to raise the dead it wouldn't go unnoticed. The one thing that scares me more than being tortured by the J-team is facing the wrath of the witches who I stole an amulet from last Halloween.

Well, that and flying monkeys. It's a thing.

Don't get the wrong idea. I'm not a thief. If you had asked me last year if I'd ever go on a road trip to Salem with a werewolf and my BFF to steal a mythological amulet, I would have said you were cuckoo for Cocoa Puffs crazy. When I learned of the spirits unleashing on Samhain, the night of Halloween, I tried to find a way to survive the spirit horde. My friends helped, but our research only turned up one thing that could protect my sanity from the evil spirits who cross through the veil on Halloween: Nera's amulet.

In a strange twist of fate, or serendipity, the amulet was sitting in an occult shop display case in Salem Village. Salem isn't far from Wakefield, one reason why our histories are intertwined. We managed to steal the amulet in time to survive the spirit storm. I should be pretty stoked about that, but I feel mostly fear and guilt.

I've been having a recurring nightmare in which the Salem witches who I stole it from come looking for their amulet. Eventually they find me, leaving behind them a wake of blood. In the dream they kill everyone I love. Each time I wake up screaming, I vow to return Nera's amulet before anything can happen to my friends.

My friends, of course, are against that idea. They worry that I won't be able to face the spirit storm on Samhain without the amulet. Evil spirits may come for me, but I have other plans. Emma has been helping me create a map of local hot spots for evil spirit activity; places where tragic deaths and murders have occurred in the past.

My plan is to arm myself with this knowledge and avoid areas where the evil spirits, the ghosts I refer to as The Grays, tend to gather. If I can find a place to hide from The Grays, then my chances of surviving Samhain are much better. Of course, there's more to my genius.

Last Samhain, I felt the calming presence of a spirit who I had helped to find the light. I think he was trying to protect me from The Grays. Since then, I've helped more spirits find peace and my hope is that all of the ghosts who I help will return to me on Samhain and defend me against evil spirits. I was already motivated to help spirits of the dead find their way into the light, but now more than ever I am trying to help every ghost that I encounter.

I'm helping people who are trapped here on earth while building an army. The job keeps me busy. It's no wonder I'm behind on my homework. Guiding lost souls is not exactly a normal extracurricular activity, but no one ever said my life was normal...or easy.

It was less difficult when I had Emma's help. She's a total research goddess. My friend, Gordy's new girlfriend, Katie, works at the library and is also great at research, but she doesn't know about my ghost problem. Gordy and Katie think I'm normal. Well, not that being totally addicted to anime and black clothing is normal, but they have no idea that I can smell the dead.

They also don't know Calvin's secret. Gordy is a great friend and I'm discovering that Katie is a total sweetheart, and less annoying than I originally thought, but there are some things best left unsaid. Cal is responsible for the safety of his people. One nervous slip of the tongue could put his entire pack in danger. That's a risk we're not yet ready to take.

Maybe someday. It would be nice to have the freedom to talk to Gordy and Katie about our troubles. With Emma too busy with her own drama, I could really use the help.

I checked my reflection one last time and shrugged. The future was coming fast, way too fast. I swear Chronos, the god of timekeeping, was messing with me. If I thought about how unprepared I was for Samhain, I'd go crazy. I need to build an army. I have to find and help as many spirits find peace as possible, before October 31st. Somehow, I also must sneak into a witch's occult shop and return Nera's amulet to its rightful owners.

But first, I have to survive high school.

Chapter 4
Calvin

I wanted to reach out and pull Yuki to my chest. I wished with all my heart that I could hold her close and shield her from the horrors of Wakefield High. But then she wouldn't be the same girl that I loved.

Yuki has always been amazing. We've been friends since elementary school and even then, she was tiny and pale, like a fragile china doll. But she was also courageous and true to herself. In the words of Mahatma Ghandi, "Strength does not come from physical capacity. It comes from an indomitable will."

Yuki never followed fads or tried to fit in even though it meant she was often left out, and always last to be picked for teams. I think the other kids at school, and in our neighborhood, were afraid of her. Yuki didn't have any friends until she met me and Emma.

Yuki also had the most terrible luck of anyone that I had ever met. She always sat in the broken chair, was given the textbook with missing pages, and if there was a single patch of ice her feet would find it.

I think what amazed me was her ability to brush it off and move on. Most kids would have cried or blamed someone else for their bad luck, but Yuki would just smile and act like nothing ever happened. I knew that I had to get to know her. She was the strongest most incredible person that I had ever met, and she still is.

I don't want to change Yuki, but lately the desire to wipe away the frown lines, as she scrunched up her white powdered forehead, was almost too strong to resist. It is hard being in love with someone like Yuki, especially for a guy with my upbringing.

Though I didn't realize it until recently, I was raised by werewolves.

My parents, and many of the other influential adults from my childhood, are members of a werewolf pack. If one member of our pack is in danger, the others rush in to help defend that individual. I am sure that this has influenced the way I react when my friends are threatened. Yuki and Emma may be human, but they are part of my pack in all the ways that matter. I would lay down my life to defend them.

But how do you protect those you love from their own thoughts and emotions? The short answer is; you don't. I can't fight all of Yuki's battles for her. In fact, she'd kick my furry butt if I tried. And deep down, I know that this problem between Emma and Yuki is about more than who Emma chooses to date.

Everything is changing, and Yuki doesn't like change. Graduation is just around the corner, a looming specter carrying a sledgehammer to smash the glass houses of our high school existence. Wakefield High has not been kind to Yuki, and though I'm sure she won't be sentimental about the daily abuse from other students, I'm also certain that she's not ready for this chapter in her life to end.

I wonder if that is the reason why she hasn't made any post-high school plans. Yuki is normally extremely proactive, almost obsessively preparing for challenges in advance, but she's the only one of our friends who doesn't have plans for after graduation.

Gordy will be going to film school to study computer animation, Katie is enrolled in an early childhood education program, Emma has been accepted to Tufts Veterinary School, and I will remain here in Maine to watch over my pack with Simon, my werewolf lieutenant, at my side. Although I don't wish to be separated from Yuki, I am concerned that she hasn't yet voiced an interest in her future.

Perhaps she still worries that there won't be one.

Yuki faced possible death and insanity when the veil between worlds thinned last Samhain. While the rest of Wakefield bobbed for apples, walked the hedge maze of horror, and went door to door trick-o'-treating for candy, Yuki, Emma, Simon, and I turned my cabin into a bunker against an army of hungry spirits.

We survived last Samhain together, but what will happen to Yuki when we are all living apart?

Chapter 5
Emma

"I have to go," I said, grabbing my bag and car keys. "I'm going to be late."

"You could play hooky with a painfully handsome werewolf," Simon said, smirking and waggling his eyebrows.

"Why would I do that?" I said while adjusting my soy cream colored scarf. "I like school. Well, the learning part, anyway. Plus, I have to keep perfect attendance between now and graduation. I'm lucky they're letting me accept my diploma this year, considering all of the days I missed after the accident."

So much had changed since that night when Yuki and I had sped off to Witchtrot Road in search of answers. I felt a pang of regret that we still weren't talking to each other. I love Yuki, but she is the most bullheaded, dogged, pigheaded...gah! Now she has me abusing the names of poor innocent animals.

"You may be the only woman alive to turn me down so cruelly," he said, pseudo-gasping and grabbing at his chest. "How shall I go on living?"

"Oh my god, Simon," I said. I rolled my eyes at him, but a treacherous smile reached my lips. "You are such a drama queen."

"King," he said.

"Whatever," I said, kissing him on the cheek. I knew better than to kiss Simon on the lips when I was in a hurry. "I have to go."

"Farewell, my queen," he said, waving. "Adieu!"

"See you after school," I said, rushing for the cabin door.

"I wouldn't miss it for the world," he said.

I could feel his eyes on my back, like scorching hot embers, as I closed the door and walked across a bed of pine needles to my car. My cheeks warmed and my grin widened as I sat behind the wheel. I knew Simon would be the first thing I saw as I exited the building at the end of the school day.

We could catch up on kisses then.

Chapter 6
Yuki

I was glad to escape the cloying truck interior. I hadn't realized how strong the wet dog smell had become until I sucked in a breath of exhaust-tinged air. Cal must be really worried about something.

Maybe he had a test today? We all had final exams next week, our last scholarly obligation before graduating, but some of the teachers were squeezing our brains dry with last minute tests and quizzes. *Sadists.*

I squeezed Cal's hand and bumped hips. That brought a grin to his lips and the wet dog smell diminished.

Cal is much better at keeping his wolf under wraps than just a few months ago. He's gained an amazing amount of control over his wolf spirit since that horrible night last fall. I still shudder when I remember just how close he came to having his secret discovered because of my actions. I know that it wasn't my fault. My brain accepts that, but my heart rebels.

It had all happened at the homecoming dance, a night that should have been a fun escape from smelly ghosts and looming Samhain worries. Without yet knowing my power to call Cal's wolf through dance, I strode out onto the dance floor and stomped out some killer moves. They were nearly killer in a very bad way. Calling Cal's wolf caused him to transform—risking potential violence, exposing his secret, and jeopardizing the pack's safety.

It was the worst night of my life. Considering how terrifying Samhain was, that's saying a lot. With Emma's help, we managed to sneak Cal out of the school dance, into her car, and to the cabin behind Cal's house. Unfortunately, shapeshifting werewolves don't travel well inside moving vehicles. Cal broke his arm, but it could have been much worse. We were lucky.

After that night, Simon began training Cal to control his wolf and helped me to understand my connection with the dead, with Cal's wolf spirit, and with my spirit guide. None of us wanted another night like the homecoming dance. But controlling a strong wolf spirit isn't easy, and Cal has more stress than most guys his age. As alpha he has responsibilities to his pack, something I know he worries about. He also, like me, had to survive these last weeks of high school. It's amazing he doesn't turn furry, like, every five minutes.

Cal's newfound control and easy smile were both monumental. Too bad I couldn't celebrate by kissing those luscious grinning lips.

Instead, I turned my attention to the social battlefield. It wouldn't pay to be distracted when threats like the J-team could be lurking inside any one of the cars parked between us and the school entrance. Walking across the parking lot set my teeth on edge. The jingling of my multi-buckled boots, chain bracelets, and protection charms attracted attention. I met each stare with a brittle smile. Thank the gods I don't have to do this much longer.

Usually, I can skip across the pavement like I have springs in the soles of my stompy boots and helium balloons attached to my black beribboned hair. But now there were chinks in my emotional armor, and I had no idea how to repair the fissures.

My heart, always so strong in the past, was like the fishnet stockings that clung to my legs—torn, shredded, and full of gaping holes.

Chapter 7
Emma

Tires squealed as I swung my car into the allotted parking spot. Only a few stragglers remained outside the school doors. A familiar shaggy head towered over a petite girl dressed in black.

Great. Just freaking awesome. If I wanted to beat the tardy bell and the potential black mark on my school record, I was going to have to enter the building alongside Cal and Yuki. Not my favorite peeps at the moment.

I grabbed my bag with shaking hands, took a deep breath, and stepped out of the car. No way was I letting the whole ex-BFF awkwardness mess up my chances for college. Plus, how bad could it be?

I've faced down corporate jerks and their security teams multiple times while protesting for animal rights. I never let those monsters get under my skin, so why worry about facing Yuki?

"Becaussse ssshe's your bessst friend," a little voice in my head answered. It sounded suspiciously like a snake.

Snakes started being able to talk to me a few months ago. It still freaks me out. I like snakes and all, but having them speak directly into my brain was so not normal. At first, it had helped me to understand how Yuki felt about sensing ghosts and getting messages from her dung beetle spirit guide—not that it helped me understand her current behavior.

I did wish she'd get over herself and start talking to me again, if only so I could ask if she too had developed a habit of giving her inner self a voice like her spirit guide. With Yuki out of the picture, and Cal keeping his distance, Simon was the only person left who I could talk to about all of this creepy supernatural stuff.

I knew that Simon would understand, he's been aware of the voice of his wolf spirit since childhood, but I didn't want to ruin the time we spent together. No, my time with Simon was an escape from all of my worries. For now, I wanted to keep it that way.

I would just have to get used to the sibilant voice in my head. *No problem. Easssy peasssy.*

I strode between cars, keeping my head down and moving as fast as I could without actually running. Maybe Yuki and Cal wouldn't even notice me if I didn't do anything to attract attention.

"Hey," Gordy called. "Emma! Cal! Yuki! Wait up!" Gordy was crossing the parking lot toward us with Katie on his arm. They were both smiling and Katie waved at us as Gordy walked toward me and nodded at Cal. "Hey, man, you guys hear the tardy bell?"

"Please say it hasn't rung yet," Katie said. "I really don't want to be grounded for graduation. I'd miss Gordy's party."

Katie's red hair was sticking out in every direction and her cheeks were flushed. Someone had been busy with some extracurricular kissing this morning. I tried to hide the grin that twitched at the corner of my mouth.

Katie and Gordy were totally cute together. I was really happy that they were dating, but running into them when Calvin and Yuki were standing there was beyond uncomfortable. Not so long ago we were all a tightly knit group of friends. Too bad someone had ripped apart the stitches that held us together, unraveling the cozy blanket of our friendship and leaving just enough strands to hang ourselves with.

I ran a finger beneath my scarf, trying to swallow. I was not going to get all weepy now. I turned to Gordy so I wouldn't have to see Yuki standing at Katie's shoulder.

"You're having a graduation party?" I asked.

"It's more of a beach party," he said, chewing on the hair that came to a point at his chin. "My uncle has a place up the coast, right on the beach. He said we can use the place the entire weekend of graduation. You're all invited. You'll come, right?"

"Um, sure," I said.

"Wouldn't miss it for the world, Gordster," Yuki said. She did one of those indecipherable handshakes with Gordy that involved fists, pinky fingers, and chest pounding. It reminded me of gorilla mating behavior.

"Of course we'll come," Calvin said. "Thanks man. You need us to bring anything?"

"No way," Katie said. "I'm making vegan, veggie, and meat-lovers snacks—something for everyone. Just bring yourself."

"And a surfboard," Gordy said. "You surf, right Cal?"

"I'm more of a hiking guy myself, but I've been known to hit the waves," he said. "It's been years though."

I tried to picture a wolf on a surfboard, and failed.

"I'm sure my uncle has a board you can use," Gory said. "He's about your size."

"Cool," Calvin said. "Um, Yuki?"

After Yuki's enthusiastic handshake with Gordy, she'd stepped back to stare at me. She looked like an angry god, displeased by her people. Her frown was deep enough to trap entire villages.

"Is she bringing someone?" Yuki asked.

Yes, I was the "she" and Yuki was pointing straight at me.

"Oh, right," Gordy said, looking from me to Yuki and back. "Of course you can bring a date if you want…"

"Never mind," I said. We were already through the school doors, so I turned my back and headed down the hall.

That went well, my sarcastic side snarked. Not that I expected it to go any better. But why did my fingers feel bruised? Looking down, I found my hands wrapped around the straps of my bag, twisting like the pale fabric was Yuki's neck.

I released the straps, smoothed out the creases, and walked to class.

Chapter 8
Yuki

I sat in class, fidgeting with the edge of my fingerless glove. The fabric was frayed, just like my nerves.

I wondered if I had nearly sabotaged Gordy's party in an effort to avoid talking about my post-graduation plans. I just knew that everyone was going to sit around a bonfire on the beach, get all sappy, and talk about how they'd miss everyone when they were gone.

Everyone was leaving me.

Dude, snap out of it! I was turning into a totally depressed jerk.

It didn't help that Emma might be there, snuggling up with Simon, while I was having my heart ripped out. I felt raw, like my skin had been rubbed off with sandpaper.

And I smelled pickles.

The golden glow of Jackson Green, a ghost who I had helped last October, hovered at my shoulder. He should have been in Heaven, or wherever spirits go when they find peace. I had helped him find his way into the light, but Jackson kept coming back.

The first time Jackson returned to me was on Samhain. He had been one of the ghosts who tried to protect me from The Grays. I knew it was him; I'd recognize that vinegar soaked smell impression anywhere.

But it wasn't Samhain today. My eyes strayed to the wall calendar beside the chalkboard, with its days crossed off in bold sharpie and graduation day circled in red, turned to the month of June. No, it was definitely not Samhain, which was at the very end of October. The veil between worlds should have kept the man's spirit where he belonged, but try telling that to Jackson.

My ghost pal had started showing up lately, whenever I was stressed. He seemed in tune with my emotions. Was I somehow calling him to me? I'd have to ask my spirit guide about that. It didn't seem right, calling a ghost to me and disturbing his rest just because I was feeling grumpy.

I scribbled a reminder in the margin of my notebook; *contact spirit guide about Mr. Pickle Pants.* If anyone other than my closest friends read that, they'd think it was some obscure anime reference. *Nope, just my bizarre life.*

Too bad hovering ghosts can't speak. I could use some good advice right now. The fact that I'd be willing to listen to the opinions of a dead guy who was murdered by his own wife showed how desperate I was.

He may not be able to speak, but Jackson and I could communicate. With my newly emerging ability to see glowing shapes of the dead, Jackson and I had developed a new means of communication. In the past, I'd create a makeshift Ouija board with the words YES, NO, and MAYBE and hope that the strength of the smell impression indicated which word a ghost was answering with. It could be accurate, but being overwhelmed by smelly ghosts was exhausting and left me with a killer headache.

Recently, I'd asked Jackson to try shining brighter to indicate his answer. Amazingly this new approach worked, and didn't leave me a moaning, drooling mess. But using my ghostly guardian as an impromptu magic eight ball seemed all shades of wrong.

I'd just have to figure out my problems on my own.

I jumped as the bell rang out. I took a deep, steadying breath and headed for the door. Once in the hallway, I braced myself for the inevitable vampire bats that swarmed inside my stomach.

"Only two weeks left," I muttered. "You can do this."

Getting to my next class meant walking past a door that filled me with dread. The memory of the things that happened behind that door still made my hands shake and my knees feel weak. The hallway seemed to shrink, closing in on me as I neared the source of my fear.

The supply closet loomed like a monster from a nightmare, growing larger as the hallway narrowed and the rest of the school fell away into a darkness so black even the humming overhead lights couldn't penetrate. The humming became a buzz as the roaring in my ears warned of a full-blown panic attack.

A little voice in my head whispered hauntingly, but managed to be heard over the incessant roaring. *Don't pass out now, girl. If you do, the J-team will get you.* Oh yeah, those thoughts were so not helping.

I shook my head, took a step closer to the door—and froze.

I knew that I should get a grip. It was just a small, messy storage room filled with the typical boxes of school supplies—no sweaty jocks or insane J-team. Not today. But the boxes of chalk and toilet paper still loomed like specters, silent witnesses to my humiliation and fear.

Did that room hold some echo of past events? One thing I've learned from my experience with the paranormal—anything is possible. If spirits of the dead can leave behind smell impressions, then why not a feeling of terror in a place where I had experienced such intense emotion?

At first, when I was abducted I had been scared, but then I got angry. Trapped and tormented by narrow-minded jerks had made me so mad, I thought my blood was boiling. The cold, emptiness…the utter terror? That came later.

Now I stood as if frozen in carbonite. Unable to run, blink, or scream. Han Solo, eat your heart out.

My body was as traitorous as Lando Calrissian.

Unlike carbonite freezing, my condition didn't cause temporary blindness. I wish that it did. I was forced to stare wide-eyed at the door that led to my darkest, most frightening nightmares. As with any bowel-churning nightmare, mine happened to feature evil jocks.

The room had been filled with members of the football team, but they were lead by the J-team. Those two were the ghouls who haunted my existence, but one of them was pure evil. Jared Zempter's threatening pose and obvious willingness to carry out any order from Jay had been terrifying enough. But the specter who tormented my dreams, and that my mind warned still lurked behind the supply closet door, was Jay Freeman.

Jay's eyes had gleamed with sadistic pleasure as meaty-hands Eddy held me down. Jay had wanted more than just answers. He had wanted to play with me, like a cat plays with a mouse. The look he had given me made my stomach churn and my skin crawl. I didn't want to be the defenseless mouse.

Jay's words from that day rang in my ears. "Yeah, freak, that's why we're here," he said. "Well, that and a little fun after." It was the "fun after" that had worried me then, and terrified me now. What if he came along and decided to finish what he had started?

No, I was not letting that creep ruin my life. Not anymore. I had sworn that day not to give up, and not to show fear. I wouldn't give the J-team the satisfaction while being held captive by the entire football team, so why start now?

A flash of heat loosed my frozen muscles and unclenched my jaw as anger burned through me. I swallowed the growing lump in my throat, blinked away tears, and bolted past the supply closet.

Nobody knew just how afraid I still was. I worked hard to smile and pretend that I was fine. But I'm far from okay. No, I'm light-years from that place. Maybe someday I'll make it there, but for now, I'm flailing around in limbo.

How did everything get so out of control?

I need to talk to Cal. I have been keeping the worst of my feelings from that day hidden, but that obviously wasn't helping anyone. Maybe talking things out will help me banish my demons, before they swallow me whole.

Chapter 9
Emma

Yuki was so wrapped up in her own mind that she didn't see me standing there. Leaning against the painted concrete wall, I watched as Yuki froze in fear and then bolted past the supply room door like it was a yawning grave trying to suck her in.

She was getting worse.

I first noticed Yuki's weird behavior two weeks ago. I had completed all of my English assignments, so my teacher gave me permission to work on the school newspaper during that period. Walking to the media room brought me past the supply closet and Yuki's daily drama.

I had no idea she'd been suffering so badly since her kidnapping. In hindsight, I was mad at myself for not recognizing the symptoms. Yuki was obviously suffering from post-traumatic stress. I'm still angry at her for abandoning our friendship, and treating Simon like garbage, but now her personality change made more sense. So what the heck do I do about it?

After the second time I caught her freaking out in the school hallway, I'd gone to the library. The books and periodicals didn't let me down. I almost wish they had.

I can still see the bold typed letters on the page of *Neuroscience*, as if the sentences burned themselves into my brain with an exceptionally wordy cattle-brand. I've petitioned and marched against the barbaric practice of branding livestock, but I felt, in the case of this metaphorical brain-brand, that I deserved the constant reminder.

According to my research, PTSD symptoms are grouped into three categories; re-experiencing symptoms, avoidance symptoms, and hyperarousal symptoms. Re-experiencing symptoms include flashbacks, bad dreams, and frightening thoughts. Avoidance symptoms can include staying away from places, people, or items that are reminders of the traumatic experience, feeling strong guilt, depression, or worry, feeling emotionally numb, losing interest in activities that were enjoyable before the trauma, feeling like you have no future, and having trouble remembering the event. Hyperarousal symptoms include feeling tense, being easily startled, having difficulty sleeping, and having angry outbursts.

After my trip to the library, I watched my former best friend more closely. Since we weren't talking to each other, I couldn't ask Yuki how she was doing. I would just have to observe. I decided to keep tailing Yuki during fourth period to see if she continued freaking out.

I secretly hoped that my suspicions were wrong and that Yuki would show the old confidence I'd come to expect from her. No such luck. Yuki exhibited all of the documented PTSD symptoms. I felt like such a jerk.

Yuki definitely had a problem. And as much as I didn't want to come face-to-face with Calvin right now, I knew what I had to do.

It was time for an intervention.

Chapter 10
Yuki

Garrett Hamlin paced at the front of the classroom, his heavy combat boots and wallet chain thumping and jingling with each lanky step. His tight black jeans and winged-skull t-shirt matched the eyeliner that rimmed sullen eyes. I used to think Garrett was totally hot, until I fell for Calvin.

Garrett wasn't hard to look at, but it turned out he was kind of a tool. According to the rumor mill, he had a paranoid streak and was prone to jealous outbursts. A few weeks ago, he accused his girlfriend of cheating on him...in red sharpie, all over her locker. *So glad I dodged that bullet.*

He continued his restless pacing, black nailed fingers flying to the ceiling as he punctuated his words. Garrett wasn't happy.

Our final project for art class was to complete a piece of art and present it to the class. Part of the presentation included a question and answer session. Garrett's sculpture wasn't bad per se, if you're into modern art, but he wouldn't tell anyone what it was. Either it was a last minute, night before creation that really didn't represent anything, or he was too paranoid to share with the class. If he didn't answer the question soon, he was going to get an F. *Dude should just make something up.*

I sighed and looked around the room. Most of the other students were texting or whispering to their friends. There were only a few students left with presentations to give. Everyone else just had to attend class. Unfortunately, I was one of the students who still had to give my presentation...and I hadn't even started work on my painting.

Every day after school, I planned on scoping out the perfect spot to paint. I had good intentions—even placed my easel and backpack filled with paints and brushes on the bench beside my front door. All that accomplished was making my dad complain about how there was nowhere to put on his shoes.

Today, I swear, I'll work on it today. I do not want to flail at the front of the class like Garrett was doing. It was embarrassing.

My pocket vibrated once. Curious, I slid my phone out and read the text. I'd probably end up with detention if caught texting in class, but watching Garrett implode was depressing. The message was from Cal.

Love you.

Luv u 2.

I really did have the best boyfriend ever. Too bad I was the worst girlfriend. Graduation was in two weeks and I still didn't have a present for Cal. *Procrastinate much?* I know it was turning into a running theme for my life. I just had no idea where to begin shopping. Something told me that Cal wouldn't like a store bought gift anyway. And working as a ghost guide to the ever-after doesn't pay so well, anyway.

I slid the phone back into my pocket and scanned the room again. This time, I noticed the artwork displayed along the walls and on a row of standing shelves. A nature landscape painting caught my eye.

Oh em gees. I totally knew what Cal's graduation gift was going to be.

Cal would love it if I made something for him with my own hands. A painting of the outdoors he loved would be the perfect gift. And I already had to create a piece of art for class. Two birds, one stone.

My dad was also going to be happy. He'd be getting his bench back.

This idea rocked.

Chapter 11
Simon

A light breeze carried the scent of stress, relief, and hormones across the parking lot. Students streamed out of the school building, yelling and cavorting in all directions, but I kept my focus on the front door, waiting for Emma.

More students appeared, girls whistling as guys tore off shirts in the summer heat. Tires squealed and stereos blared, making my wolf restless, but still I waited.

Finally, Emma stepped out into the sun—a pale goddess amidst a crowd of savages. A low growl ground past my teeth like rocks as a sweaty kid ran past Emma, hitting her shoulder and knocking her backpack to the ground, as he rushed to catch up with his friends. I clenched my jaw, resisting the urge to run to her side…or tear out his throat.

Instead, I continued to lean casually against Emma's car. After a momentary pause to glare at her assailant and retrieve her bag, Emma strode gracefully through the lingering crowds of students and speeding cars.

It still surprised me that she wasn't one of the Old Blood. Emma was human, but she moved with the sinuous grace of a wolf, or a snake.

Emma hadn't mentioned her ability to listen to snakes since the talent first emerged, but I noticed how she went rigid and cocked her head to one side whenever a snake was near. She may prefer to keep her newfound gift to herself, but I knew it continued to flummox her. Our animals, my wolf and her snake, were something we needed to discuss further. I wanted to know everything about her, and vice versa, but Emma had a way of distracting me from things like talking.

Like she was doing now.

"Kiss me," Emma said. She dropped her bag on the pavement and grabbed the front of my shirt.

"Bad day?" I asked, cocking an eyebrow at her. I wanted to fulfill her demands, but it seemed polite to ask about her day.

"The worst," she said. "No more talking."

Emma reached up, fingertips trailing teasingly along my neck, then plunging her hands into my hair as she pulled my lips onto hers. Emma may not be a werewolf, but she had her own teeth and claws—and knew how to use them.

Her fingers released as our kiss deepened, nails following a return track down my neck to follow my spine. Hands resting on my hips, Emma pulled away far enough so that our eyes met. With a mischievous smile, she nipped playfully at the scar on the edge of my lips then proceeded to drive me crazy with another long kiss. Fingernails dug into my back, arms pulling me closer.

When we finally parted, Emma trembled and I was panting like the wolf that I am. But I didn't drool, much.

"Sorry you had a bad day," I said, breathing in the scent of Emma's shampoo as I whispered into her hair.

"It's getting better," she said.

Yes, it certainly was.

Chapter 12
Yuki

Getting rid of Cal was harder than I expected. He wasn't exactly clingy, but we usually spent time together after school, especially since things with Emma went nuclear.

But today I had other plans—secret graduation prezzie type plans—that did not include Cal. I was on a mission to find the perfect spot to paint, for Cal's gift and my final project for art class. I hadn't felt this excited about anything in weeks.

I waited for Cal's truck to round the corner then skipped up the front steps. I told Cal that I had to stay home and do homework, or I was going to fail my classes and flunk out of senior year. *Hasta la vista graduation.* It wasn't a total complete lie. I was working on homework, and passing art class and graduating high school depended on completing this project, but I wasn't studying at home. It was just a teensy little white lie about where I would be spending the afternoon. No big deal.

I unlocked the front door and walked through the dark house to the kitchen. My parents were both at work. They'd be gone for at least three more hours, probably longer. I unzipped my backpack and started filling it with supplies. I may be on a mission, but even secret agents have to eat, right?

I considered tossing in a few frozen veggie burritos, but I'd have no way to cook them and they'd be gross cold. If I had a car, I could get one of those toaster ovens that plugs into the lighter and runs off the battery. That, of course, was a pipe dream. Smelling, and now seeing, ghosts is so not conducive to safe driving. I'd had more than enough brushes with death.

Nope, it was a bicycle, and a lifetime of mooching rides off my friends, for me. The burritos went back in the freezer and a bag of trail mix and two bottles of water went into my backpack. Grabbing the marker hanging from a piece of ribbon attached to a magnet on the fridge, I left a note for my parents on the dry erase board.

Working on school project, be home soon.

I retrieved the satchel holding my easel and paint and snatched a hoodie from a peg above the hall bench. When my dad came home, he'd have a place to take off his shoes. This plan was awesomesauce.

I went out the front door, locking it behind me, and waddled down the driveway with my armload of supplies. I cut across a strip of lawn and set my supplies on the grass beside my bicycle. My bike leaned against my mom's gardening shed. I strapped the easel and a small folding stool to the back.

Next, I grabbed the sides of my long skirt and tied knots into the fabric. The last thing I needed was to catch my skirt in the wheel spokes while riding. Secret agents don't going flying over their handlebars—it attracts too much attention.

I reached into my skirt pocket and turned off my phone. Secret agents also don't have loud annoying ringtones. Plus, my phone would probably go flying out my pocket the second I started pedaling, or turned a corner. I transferred it to my backpack instead. I could check in with my folks later if I was running late.

I checked the straps of my backpack and walked my bike down to the street. Looking both ways, I jumped on, my boots gripping the pedals and the wind in my face. For the first time in months, I felt like I was moving forward.

I felt like I was free.

Chapter 13
Emma

Simon wasn't overly thrilled when I dropped him off before reaching the cabin. He probably had envisioned a romantic evening together, but I needed to talk to Cal, alone.

On the ride over, I explained about Yuki's recent behavior and how I suspected she had some deep-seated issues related to her abduction. Simon raised an eyebrow at my concern over Yuki, we hadn't been acting like BFF's lately, but when I started describing her PTSD behavior he agreed that something needed to be done.

Simon could understand the potential risks of leaving a person dealing with post traumatic stress to their own devices. He understood in spades.

I had learned of Simon's battle with depression, and drug addiction, a few months ago. After we reported the Wakefield meth lab to the police, Simon and I had had our first heart to heart talk about his past. I knew he had gone through "a bad patch" after his werewolf girlfriend Meredith was shot to death. Having your girlfriend die in your arms?—definitely a PTSD inducing experience.

Unfortunately, Simon had been far from the support of his family when Meredith was shot. Simon and Meredith had traveled to England to attend college together and experience something new and different away from the pack. Instead, Meredith died and Simon was left to mourn her death in the worst way possible. He dealt with his grief, self-loathing, guilt, and growing anger by turning to drugs.

After nearly killing himself with heroin, and burning every possible bridge with his college mates, Simon finally returned to the states, and his pack. But he was forever changed. There's a darkness that can be seen behind his eyes sometimes when he thinks no one is paying attention. A pain that never healed made all the more raw by a shame he can never escape.

Simon became an addict and did things he's not proud of. But he had been all alone. He may be angry with Yuki and her exasperating recent behavior, but now that he knew the cause he would stop at nothing to prevent her from falling into the downward spiral that nearly swallowed him whole. It was time to cast aside petty arguments.

Of course, he was still disappointed that we wouldn't be spending our afternoon kissing. Simon stood there pouting in my rearview mirror before moving into the trees. Poor guy, he has to go let his wolf run, and cool off.

I smiled a wicked grin and followed the dirt track to the cabin. I'd make it up to Simon later over dinner. He offered to meet at my favorite vegetarian restaurant in town, so I knew he was eager for our date. I just hoped that Cal would have a plan for helping Yuki.

My grin faded as I got out of my car. Cal's truck was parked outside, but I didn't know if he was alone. I should have called ahead, but I'd been distracted by my worry for Yuki, and kissing Simon. If Yuki was inside, my plan would fall apart like a bride stranded at the altar.

I shook my head. I was graduating next week. I was so not thinking about weddings. What the heck was wrong with me? Maybe back in fourth grade Yuki had been right; boy cooties really do melt your brain.

I lifted my chin and strode to the door. I knocked, hard, using the code we'd established for pack emergencies. Yuki may be human, but according to Cal, she was a member of his pack and she was in trouble. Hopefully he wouldn't fault my logic.

We'd come up with the coded knocks in case someone was busy kissing inside. A regular knock could be ignored, but a pack knock was more important than making out.

The door swung open exposing Cal's flushed face. I glanced into the small room behind him, but he was alone. Good. For once, I was in luck.

"Can I come in?" I asked.

"Sure, sorry, come on in," Cal said.

I walked over to the couch and sat, waiting for Cal. He ran a hand through shaggy hair as he shut the door. With a heavy sigh, he turned to face me. Worry lines etched the skin around his eyes and his mouth, usually so quick to smile, was set in a grim line.

"You used the pack 911 knock," he said. "What's happened?"

"Come over and sit down," I said.

"I'd rather stand," he said.

He paced the short length of the room, the hem of his jeans collecting dust as his bare feet stirred up a small cloud of dirt and animal hair. You could tell werewolf boys lived here.

I stopped watching Cal's feet and met his worried eyes with my own.

"It's Yuki," I said. "I think she's in trouble."

The color drained from Cal's tanned face, like pouring too much soy milk into coffee.

"On second thought," he said. "I'll sit."

Chapter 14
Calvin

I couldn't believe what Emma was telling me, and yet the evidence had been there all along. How could I have been so blind?

"If you don't blink soon, I'm force feeding you one of my teas," Emma said.

That snapped me out of my funk. Emma's herbal teas and tinctures may help heal wounds, but they tasted awful. I wouldn't risk drinking one unless suffering from a serious injury.

Too bad she didn't have a tea for healing a broken heart.

I thought I'd been a good boyfriend, but now I was beginning to wonder. How could I have been so unaware of what Yuki was going through?

I should have known it would be terrifying to walk that hallway every day to class. I could have offered to walk her past the supply closet door, so she didn't have to endure the fear alone. I would have changed my class schedule to be there for her. But I hadn't been there for her, hadn't even noticed that something was wrong.

Should have, could have, would have—never helped anyone at all. I was slipping back into a depressed stupor, focusing on the past, but Yuki needed me now. We had to figure out how to help her before things got any worse.

I rubbed my face briskly.

"What do you propose we do?" I asked.

Emma would have a plan, she always had a plan. She probably went to the library and spent hours doing research before coming here. She'd know what to do.

"I have no idea," she said.

My stomach twisted and depression was replaced by fear.

"You said she has classic PTSD symptoms," I said. "Did you read that in a book?"

"Yes, and a medical journal," she said.

The claws in my gut stopped their twisting. Emma may be dating my roommate, but she hadn't changed one bit. For some reason, that gave me hope.

"Okay, so we need to find out what those books recommend we do to help a person with PTSD," I said. "Do you remember anything?"

"They said to let the person know that they can talk about the traumatic event, and to help them get professional counseling," she said. "Talking is important."

Emma explained the symptoms of PTSD and the need for discussing the traumatic event and rebuilding trust.

"Good, I'll go over there now," I said. I stood, grabbing my keys. "I'll try to get Yuki talking about what happened to her."

"What should I do?" Emma asked.

Emma bit her lip and her hands fidgeted with a long strand of hair. I was glad that Emma was worried about Yuki. They may be fighting, but at least Emma still cared.

"I'll call you later," I said. "Hopefully, by the time I call, everything will have sorted itself out. I'm sure Yuki will agree to counseling once she realizes just how serious this is."

I sounded more confident than I felt. Yuki was stubborn, and even I'd noticed her flashes of anger lately. I'd chalked them up to graduation jitters, but now that I knew how common angry outbursts were for people with PTSD, I worried about how badly Yuki's fear was eating her up inside. Would she agree to counseling, or lash out?

"Okay, I'm having dinner with Simon later, but call any time," she said. "I'll keep my ringer on. And Cal? Don't hesitate to call for backup. I know how Yuki can get when she's upset. Sometimes she just needs a hot bath and a good cry."

"Thanks," I said.

Emma nodded once and walked out the door.

I grabbed my shoes and started pulling them on, rushing to tie the laces. The door creaked open again and I looked up to see Simon lope in.

He'd been for a run. His hands and feet were caked with mud and small pieces of grass and leaves clung to his hair.

"Hey, I'm on my way out," I said. "I need to go see Yuki, but, man, you may want to try talking to Emma later. She seems really worried."

"Maybe you should focus on your own love life before giving other people advice," he said.

Simon ground the words through clenched teeth while his wolf danced behind his eyes. It may not be the full moon, but strong emotions could bring our wolves to the surface. But Simon usually had more control. It would take more than an off the cuff remark to force Simon's wolf to the surface.

Something else must be preying on his mind. Best diffuse the situation by apologizing. I didn't have time for a fight with Simon. I needed to go see Yuki.

"Look, I'm sorry," I said. "I'm worried about Yuki."

"You should be worried, mate," he said.

Simon looked me straight in the eye, something most werewolves don't do now that I am alpha. He was serious.

"What do you mean by that?" I asked.

"I know how you and Yuki disapprove of my relationship with Emma," he said. "You say it's because I'm older. There may be an age gap between us, but at least I'm not holding her back."

My mouth went dry and my stomach twisted as the bottom fell out of my happy little world. Was I really holding Yuki back? Would she be better off without me?

Before Emma's revelation, I wouldn't have believed it. I would have told Simon to go cool off. But pieces of the puzzle were falling together and it was all happening so fast. It was like being trapped inside an expert level of Tetris.

The sky was falling and I had no idea where to run, or how to protect the one I love.

Chapter 15
Yuki

I angled my bike toward the park, enjoying the way the afternoon sun's rays cut through the planted trees lining the path. The golden glow reminded me of contented ghosts. I smiled and pedaled faster.

I hoped to find a nice outdoor location for my painting. Cal loved nature and the outdoors. But I wasn't a big fan of traipsing through thick woods—mosquitoes, black flies, and spiders, oh my!—so I chose the park.

Of course, Wakefield Park was huge. I came to a halt just inside the park entrance. A duck pond surrounded by benches lay to my right, trails branched off to my left, and a series of sports fields and tennis courts lay just beyond the small amphitheater on the path straight ahead.

I was going to hurry to the benches around the duck pond, but the heady scent of roses filled my head. I swayed on my feet, struggling to keep my bicycle upright. I looked around, ignoring the spinning in my head, but there were no rose bushes in sight.

An aching pressure grew beneath my temples and I winced. This was no ordinary scent. A ghost lingered in this park and I was sensing the smell impression that their spirit had left behind.

The smell impression was complicated, rose fragrance mixed with two other scents. But the smell of roses was definitely the strongest and most easily identifiable.

A second scent reminded me of a sweater my mom made for me when she was going through her knitting phase. The sweater hung lower on one side and the collar was really too small for my head to fit through, but it was wearable. I grinned at the memory.

My mom was always trying some new hobby to fill her one day off each week. Don't even get me started on her glue-gun phase—that was a total nightmare. The knitting wasn't too terrible, but the yarn she used for that sweater was some kind of natural handspun, hand dyed wool that smelled funny. I worried that it made me smell like wet dog, though I guess it really was more like oily sheep.

That's right. Mom said the smell was from lanolin, natural oil found on sheep wool. I was definitely sensing a ghost and it smelled like roses and lanolin…and something else.

The third smell was harder to place. I closed my eyes and used a yoga breathing Cal had taught me, and the focusing techniques Simon had drilled into my head, to center my thoughts on the smell impression. Bird song faded as everything dropped away, leaving only the ghost and its complicated smell.

An acrid chemical smell itched at my nose. It had a slight vinegar-like odor, but it definitely wasn't the pure vinegar scent of Jackson's ghost. The third scent may not be Jackson, but the smell was familiar. I spread out my awareness, trying to take in more of the smell impression.

I was like a sommelier at a wine tasting, breathing in the psychic sent and rolling it along the tongue. If I let my concentration slip and thought about how gross it was to have a ghost in my mouth, I'd probably vomit. This part of working with ghosts was totally gag-worthy.

But I was getting better at it.

My mad ghost smelling skills finally unearthed the mystery scent. The chemical smell with a slight vinegar tang reminded me of the school darkroom. I had been in there often enough with Emma and Gordy to recognize the smell, but couldn't be sure if it indicated developer or stop bath chemicals. Either way, I now knew more than I did before.

This ghost had some connection to photography. *Interesting.*

"Hey, Rose," I whispered. The ghost smelled mostly of roses, so Rose it is. Well, until I find out what its real name was. "Do you need help?"

Stupid question. My head filled with the cloying scent of roses and I wretched. Of course it needed help. It was a ghost.

I gripped the handlebars of my bike with sweating hands and pushed down the urge to hurl. Okay, Yuki. Just figure out what the smelly ghost wants. Then it's painting time.

"Um, can you back off just a little?" I asked. "I can't help you if I pass out."

The weight on my lungs lifted and clean air rushed in. I opened my eyes to see a golden shimmer hovering above a trail to my left. There you are.

"Okay, I'll try to follow you," I said.

The glow brightened and the smell increased. Apparently, that was exactly what the spirit wanted to hear.

My boots found their way onto the pedals again and I started down the shadowed hiking path, leaving the duck pond behind.

Chapter 16
Simon

"Back off," Calvin growled.

"Is that an order?" I asked.

I could feel my lip curl as my wolf gnashed its teeth. Over the past few weeks, I had watched Emma become more and more upset as her friends betrayed her, as my alpha betrayed me, with their harsh disapproval.

Yuki and Calvin were supposedly the perfect bloody couple who no one else could possibly equal, until now. Well they set the bar too sodding high now didn't they? The two soul mates who had been judgmental of our relationship from the start had their own issues. Yuki was suffering and Calvin, who claimed to be so in tune with her feelings, had no idea.

I had been struggling with my feelings for weeks and now I had an outlet for my bottled up anger. I was itching for a fight.

"No," Calvin said, shaking his head. "No it's not an order. I'm sorry. I don't want to fight you."

If he wouldn't fight, then I had to run. I needed to feel the wind on my face...and blood on my muzzle.

I stalked away, nearly taking the door off its hinges in my rush to get outdoors and unleash my wolf. I shifted in a flash of silver fur, bones aching as I hurried the transformation. I ran into the woods, away from Calvin, away from Yuki, and away from the reminders of my tormented past.

Spittle formed at my mouth and flew behind me as the wind hit my face. I raced through the forest, dodging trees and boulders at deadly speed. I should slow down. Braining myself on a rock or tree wouldn't do me any good, but my wolf spirit wanted to run and I was too upset to wrestle him back into submission.

No, my wolf wasn't who I wanted to fight. I grinned, the air cool on my exposed teeth. I wouldn't attack Calvin, of course, but I was in no shape for my dinner date with Emma. She already drove me crazy—her wry smile, her hair, her smell—there was no way that I could meet her like this. I was going to have to blow off some steam.

I needed to hunt.

I caught the scent of a white-tailed deer and pushed myself to run faster. I grinned so widely that all now all of my teeth were exposed to the wind. All the better to eat you with *my deer*.

Emma would kill me if she found out about my pre-dinner snack. She didn't approve of killing animals for food and wouldn't appreciate the thrill of the hunt that already pushed adrenaline through my veins.

I slowed, grin faltering, but shook my head. Sod it. A man has needs, right?

I licked my lips and nose and continued my pursuit.

Chapter 17
Calvin

*S*imon's angry words continued to ring in my ears. *She's better off without you, mate.*

I needed to go to Yuki and confront her about Emma's fears. I had to know if she was okay. But did I really have the right to dredge up that nightmare moment from her past? Was I the best person for the job? Or was I, as Simon stated, holding her back?

I thought that I was good for Yuki, and her for me, but had I been the only one to reap the benefits?

I tried to look at my relationship with Yuki objectively. She'd been placed in the face of danger more than once because of me. When I couldn't control my wolf, I came close to tearing Yuki and Emma apart. Later, when a deranged werewolf began hunting his own kind, Yuki again got caught in the cross-fire. And when she was in a horrible accident, I did nothing to help.

Sure, I lent her my support and love, but that wasn't enough. Maybe, it never would be.

I sighed and shook my head. Sulking and worrying over Simon's words wasn't helping Yuki. I pulled out my phone and hit speed dial, needing to hear her voice. But the call went to voicemail.

That was strange. Yuki almost always had her cell on, even in class. With her parents working late, it would be foolish not to keep her phone with her. She was alone in that old house. What if she fell down the stairs or slipped on the bathroom floor?

Worry stabbed my chest and made my blood run cold. I grabbed my keys and ran to my truck.

Chapter 18
Yuki

My teeth clacked together as I rode my bike over a large tree root. It was dumb luck that I didn't go flying over the handlebars. I slowed, letting my boots drag across the gravel path overgrown with weeds and grass.

The shimmering form of Rose, the fragrant ghost I was following, continued to flit over the trail at breakneck speed. Good for the impatient ghost, but not so good for those of us who still had physical bodies that could be injured.

"Wait up!" I yelled.

The ghost came to a halt, but bounced up and down in what I imagined was big time agitation. Jeesh, ghosts are all the same. They discover that I can sense them and then they're all, me, me, me.

I brushed an arm across my forehead, wiping away beads of sweat that were starting to run into my eyes. Great, now I was all sweaty and gross. I looked down at my sleeve. The once black fabric was now covered in a pasty mixture of white face powder and perspiration.

"I could so go for a bubble bath right now," I muttered.

Instead I puffed out a sigh, blowing black bangs out of my face, and started pedaling again up the trail. I had to struggle to keep up with my ghost trail guide who took off as soon as I started moving. Its golden glow disappeared around a corner and I had to stand on the pedals to pick up more speed.

"So much for waiting for me," I grumbled.

I had no idea how far these trails went on for. We had already left the familiar open grassy areas and easy foot paths of the park behind. Gnarled old trees marched closer to the trail, leaving a narrow track just large enough for two people to run abreast. With my overburdened bicycle laden with easel, paints, and enough food for an army, I hoped that I wouldn't meet anyone else on the trail. Though in this heat, that probably wasn't likely.

So far, I hadn't seen a living soul.

Pedaling fast to catch up to my spectral guide, I gulped in air and coughed as I swallowed a bug. Yep, my psychic gift royally sucked.

Eyes watering, I careened around the corner and nearly ran into a boulder. Stones littered the ground—some covered in moss while others lay bare, bleached by the sun like old bones.

The ghost was hovering a few yards away beside a high stone wall. The wall was old and crumbling in places. Perhaps the remnants of a Victorian garden in decay. It was my kind of place.

One end of the wall was little more than a pile of fallen stones, while the other end was covered in climbing roses. The fragrant red blossoms were reminiscent of the ghost's own signature scent, sans lanolin and darkroom chemicals.

As I approached, trying to look over the wall that towered above my head, the ghost came to sparkle and twinkle beside the rose bush. The golden spirit aura and scarlet flowers made a hauntingly beautiful picture. Cal would love it. With a little help from beyond, I'd found the perfect painting spot.

I set the kickstand and stepped off my bike, slowly moving toward the ghost. It didn't stray from its spot beside the roses.

I wasn't sure why the ghost had led me here, but it couldn't hurt to examine the scene with an artist's eye. Sometimes when I looked at a drawing or painting after completion, I saw details that I hadn't truly noticed were there. Perhaps painting would actually help me solve this case and help the ghost find its way into the light.

There was only one way to find out.

Chapter 19
Emma

As usual, Simon was late. I picked at my quinoa and shallot salad appetizer and checked my phone for the bazillionth time. No messages.

This wasn't the first time Simon lost track of time, but it still hurt. Had he forgotten our dinner date at the café?

Just Veggin' wasn't fancy, but I loved this place. It was on the opposite side of town from Mr. Green Genes, the organic, fair trade, non-GMO restaurant where I used to go nearly every day with Yuki. I still like the food at Green Genes, but it seemed somehow wrong hanging out there with Simon. It was Yuki's favorite place, home of the famous veggie burritos she loved so much. The last time I went there, the food just stuck in my throat. I haven't been back since.

At Green Genes everything in the place is green—the tabletops, booths, floor, walls were all different shades of green. Here at Just Veggin' the owners had taken a more lively approach to decorating. Every surface was a different color and the walls were covered in splashes of primary colors, like the result of an epic fruit and veggie food fight.

I turned my attention from the brightly painted walls and focused on the television above the juice bar. The six o'clock news was replacing old sitcom reruns. They'd start with boring local news first, but if I had to wait much longer for Simon I might catch an update on congressional deliberations over new animal cruelty laws.

"Gina, can you turn that up?" I asked the waitress.

It was a weeknight and the place wasn't busy. I didn't think she'd mind.

Gina glanced at the empty chair across from me and gave me a sympathetic grin.

"Sure, sugar," she said. "Want to go ahead and order your dinner or you still want to wait?"

"I'll wait," I said.

Gina shrugged and went over to a mug on the juice bar that held the television remote. She turned up the volume and perched on a stool, her purple and green hair matching the iridescent birds painted on a faux-grass canopy above her head.

The juice bar was made to look like a Tiki bar. It was one of the reasons why Yuki didn't like coming here. The smiling monkeys swinging from the ceiling gave her the creeps.

"This just in," the female newscaster said. "Wakefield police have issued a warning to all residents to use caution after the report of a missing local teenager. Parents of Sarah Randall, a freshman at Wakefield High School, have offered a reward for information leading to her safe return. A press conference is scheduled later this evening. Our man on the ground, Tom Desker, reports that residents remain diligent as fears of the Graduation Grabber return to Wakefield after a five year hiatus."

The school pictures of two high school girls flashed on the screen.

"The last case involving the Grabber happened five years ago when Wakefield students Michelle Ouellette and Rose Peterson went missing. The body of Rose Peterson was never found, but police confirmed that Michelle Ouellette was murdered in the same manner as four other teens over a three year period."

The blond newscaster replaced the pictures of the missing school girls, her tight smile seeming inappropriate as she recounted the deaths of local teens. Why do newscasters always have to look so happy?

"The disappearance of Sarah Randall has Wakefield residents worried that the Grabber may have returned to this small community. Has the Graduation Grabber emerged from hiding? Where has he been and what has he been doing over the past five years? Join us as we explore these questions and more this evening. Be sure to tune in to our News at Ten update."

"Who's the Graduation Grabber?" Simon asked.

I jumped and nearly toppled my banana flax smoothie.

"Oh em gees, Simon!" I said. "Don't do that. You scared the heck out of me."

He grinned, his scar jumping as a laugh rumbled deep in his throat. The sound made my cheeks go warm.

"You're cute when you're scared, love," he said.

"Well, of course I freaked a little," I said, pointing at the television. "You just snuck up on me while they announced the Graduation Grabber might be back."

"The Graduation Grabber?" he asked.

He slid into the empty seat across from me and stretched out his legs, leaning back in his chair. His body language was relaxed, but I saw his eye twitch before raising a brow at me. Simon was a werewolf and wolves were always protective of their pack, and their mate. If Simon thought I was in danger, he'd do anything to keep me safe.

I can take care of myself, but knowing how Simon felt made me feel all warm and happy. It was good to know that even with the Graduation Grabber in town, I was perfectly safe. Even if the Grabber was a total freak who liked to kidnap and murder high school girls the week before graduation.

"The Graduation Grabber is the name the press gave the guy they think abducted and murdered all of those girls," I said. I was talking too fast and my hands danced in the air like over-caffeinated butterflies. With an effort, I shoved my hands under my legs and tried to slow down.

"How many girls?" Simon asked, suddenly serious.

"Six girls went missing, two each year around graduation," I said. "They were all high school students and female. But only five bodies were found. The police think Rose Peterson was the sixth victim, since the Grabber always abducted two girls each year and she went missing a few days before graduation. But her body was never found."

"And now one girl, a high school student, has gone missing in Wakefield a week before graduation," Simon said.

My bag started ringing and I jumped. Talking about the Graduation Grabber was making me jittery. Maybe we should just order dinner and change the subject.

"Yes, that's why the media is speculating about the Grabber," I said, distracted. I pulled out my phone and checked the screen. It was Calvin. "Sorry, I have to take this."

Calvin was pretty upset when I saw him last. I had just dropped the bomb that Yuki might be suffering from PTSD and her behavior was getting more erratic. I could still remember the fear in her eyes when she froze in front of the supply closet today at school.

Maybe Calvin had an update. I could use some good news right now.

Chapter 20
Calvin

I drove to Yuki's in a cloud of worry and indecision. Emma seemed convinced that Yuki was suffering from PTSD and needed help. And Simon's angry outburst still rang in my ears. I needed to be reassured that Yuki was okay, that we were okay.

But the house looked empty.

I pulled the truck alongside the potting shed and jumped out. The windows were dark, like a skull's empty eye sockets staring at me as I rushed up the front steps. I knocked and rang the doorbell, but the sounds echoed inside without a response. No heavy boots clomping down the stairs. No happy shout from Yuki's room.

I went back down the steps and knelt in the mulch beneath an overgrown evergreen bush. My hand finally found the plastic hide-a-key and I had to choke back a laugh. The Stennings didn't have a dog, but Yuki had picked the dog poop shaped hide-a-key with the logic that no burglar in their right mind would touch it.

I retrieved the key and rushed back up the steps, jamming it into the lock. The door hit the wall as I thrust it open, eyes looking in every direction. No Yuki.

"Yuki!" I yelled.

No response.

I stuck my head in the kitchen, but it was empty. Running back through the living room and up the stairs, I peeked into her parents' bedroom and the guest room. Nobody was home. I knocked one more time on Yuki's bedroom door and pushed it open with a creak of the hinges. The bed lay empty.

My earlier worry that Yuki may have fallen in the bathroom returned and I rushed across the room. The door to the bathroom hung open, towels hanging on their rungs, shampoo on the shelf above the tub. Nothing was out of order, but the room was empty.

Yuki wasn't home.

But that didn't make any sense. Yuki had said she couldn't hang out after school because she had to stay home and finish her homework. Since she didn't drive, it was unlikely that Yuki would have just walked off. If she needed something from the library, she would have called for a ride.

Her behavior didn't make any sense. But wasn't that what Emma had been talking about? PTSD could cause erratic behavior. Was this another symptom?

Was I too late?

Maybe Emma would know what to do. She had read the library books and journal articles. Plus, maybe she'd seen Yuki in town. It was a long shot, but I was running out of ideas…and starting to panic.

My wolf was already struggling to break free. I took a few controlling breaths before dialing Emma.

"Emma, I need your help," I said when she picked up. "Yuki's missing."

"Oh my God," Emma said. She muttered "it's Calvin" to someone, probably Simon. "Are you near a TV?"

I grunted the affirmative. Yuki had a small television perched on the edge of a vanity table, but it was rarely used. The TV was covered in black scarves, boot laces, and knit arm warmers. I started brushing these aside.

"Turn it on, and sit down," she said. "You're going to need to see this."

I grabbed the remote, covered in pink and black smiling skull and crossbones stickers, and hit power. The screen on Yuki's TV came to life. She only got three channels on her bedroom television, but I didn't have to go channel surfing. A news alert was scrolling at the bottom of the screen and two tearful parents were standing at a podium pleading for the return of their daughter.

It wasn't Yuki's parents. Thank God.

The news took a moment to sink in. The Graduation Grabber had returned to Wakefield. He'd already abducted one girl and, if things went like the events of five years ago, there would be a second girl soon.

"Emma?" I croaked. I coughed trying to clear my throat. "We have to find Yuki."

"I know," she said. "I can't believe she's missing."

"She told me she'd be home working on homework," I said, trying to lasso my stampeding thoughts.

"I'll check the library," Emma said. "Yuki said she was doing homework, right? She's probably there. I'll call Gordy and Katie on the way. If Katie's working, she can start searching the library before I get there."

"Is Simon with you?" I asked. Emma had mentioned a dinner date.

Yes," said.

I could hear her teeth hit together as she bit off the word. She didn't like me bringing up Simon, but I needed his help. If we couldn't find Yuki here in town, we'd need to track her scent in the surrounding mountain foothills and forest. There were few wolves as skilled at tracking as Simon.

"Good, put him on," I said.

"Okay, I'll call if I find anything," she said.

"Fine way to spoil my dinner date," Simon said. "If I didn't know better, mate, I'd say you lot planned this."

"Give me a break, Simon," I said. I sighed and ran my free hand through my hair, tugging so hard it was surprising I didn't have bald tracks along my scalp. Simon was always exasperating, I figured he was the universe's way of testing me, but this was getting ridiculous. As Yuki would say, he needed to get over himself. "Yuki's missing and the Graduation Grabber is in town. If Emma were in the same situation, I'd be at your side, man, asking what I could do to help."

"Touché," he said. "What do you need?"

"I need you to be my eyes, ears, and nose on the street," I said. I stared out the window, coming up with a plan. "I'll check the west side of town, you take the east. Try to catch Yuki's scent."

"And if I find her?" he asked. "What then? Emma seems to think the girl's gone off her rocker."

"Improvise," I said. "Just keep her safe."

Chapter 21
Yuki

The collapsible stool I brought with me felt like it was becoming a permanent part of my butt and my right foot had fallen asleep. I should probably get up and stretch my legs, but I didn't know how long the ghost would remain positioned by the stone wall.

I leaned down to reach into the satchel holding my art supplies where it sat beside the stool and pulled out more paint. I grabbed the palette knife with tired, aching fingers and scraped the colors together until I had more of the red needed to finish painting the scarlet roses that climbed the stone wall.

I squinted at the ghost's golden aura. That was strange. I pinched the bridge of my nose and rubbed my eyes with the backs of my hands. The ghost seemed to be glowing brighter.

Blinking, I examined the colors on the canvas and compared them to the scene in front of me. Oh, the ghost wasn't glowing brighter. The clearing where I sat was getting darker. I looked up above the treetops and confirmed that the sun was sitting lower in the sky. I'd have to work more quickly if I wanted to complete the painting before dark.

I didn't really want to be out in these woods after nightfall. I was a long way from the well-groomed trails near the park entrance. Riding my bike on these trails would be foolish in the dark. With my luck, I'd end up head first in a thorn bush or hit in the face by a low branch.

At least I'd brought flashlights. Ever since our adventure in the caves, looking for a missing werewolf, I never left home without one, or three. That night still gave me nightmares. The caves were dark and confusing, but we eventually found the missing teen, and a psychotic werewolf killer. A chill crept up my spine making me shiver.

I grabbed a flashlight from my bag and held it tight in my fist.

We had helped bring the killer into custody. He remained a ward of a pack therapist, living in the werewolf equivalent of a halfway house. There was nothing to be afraid of. No psychotic werewolves out here.

Just me and a smelly ghost.

Chapter 22
Simon

"Troublesome girl," I muttered.

I wiped a piece of stinking refuse off my custom leather boots and dropped the soiled handkerchief into a dumpster. Most werewolves disdained material things, preferring a simple back-to-nature lifestyle. I shuddered at the thought. I may enjoy a good run through the woods while in wolf form, but as a man I appreciated the nicer things in life.

Unfortunately, the residents of this street seemed to have an overzealous appreciation for cheap wine and fast food. The place reeked of grease and garbage.

I was in another alley. This one ran behind the Gas N Gulp, Douggie's Fried Chicken, and Wok On In, a Chinese takeaway. I searched beneath the piles of damp cardboard boxes and plastic milk crates, but all I found was a cockroach and an old coat soaked in urine.

No Yuki. For that, I was grateful. I may be mad at the girl, but I didn't want to find her here in the alley strung out on drugs or the latest victim of the Graduation Grabber.

I was, however irritated that while I searched for Yuki, Emma was left unprotected. I wanted to be by her side, keeping her safe from this killer. But Calvin had requested my help in the search for Yuki, and Emma had insisted on looking for her in the library.

At least Emma wasn't alone.

I had waited for her to meet up with Gordy and Katie before beginning my search for Yuki. They promised to stick together. I had to trust that there was safety in numbers. Otherwise I'd become insane with worry.

I swallowed the howl that rose up in my throat.

Emma would never forgive me if I let her best friend die because I was too worried about her own safety. They may be fighting at the moment, but Emma's worry for Yuki was real. I suspected that if something happened to Yuki now, Emma would never forgive herself for allowing her friend to suffer the after effects of her abduction alone.

No, I had to find Yuki before anything dire could happen to the girl. Knowing Yuki's luck, I better hurry. That girl attracts trouble like I attract women.

I exited the alley and ran to my motorcycle. I needed to ride to the outskirts of town where I could shift into wolf form. Trying to catch Yuki's scent in a sea of sweating humans, vehicle exhaust, and rotting garbage was getting me nowhere.

I kicked the bike into gear and hit the throttle. It roared and jumped out into traffic, leaving a strip of black rubber behind. I wove between cars and around trucks hauling boats and campers. I cursed at the summer traffic that came early with this week's heat wave.

At the next light, I used the empty turning lane to pass half a dozen vehicles waiting their turn. Horns blared and more than one driver sent up a one fingered salute. I rode on without responding in kind.

I didn't have time to waste.

Chapter 23
Emma

The library is my favorite place in Wakefield, but today the shadows between shelving, and behind desks and work tables, felt ominous. I never realized just how many places there were to hide, or disappear.

"OhmygoshIcan'tbelieveit," Katie said, for the thousandth time.

I liked Katie, but her nervous tendency for rapid speech was making me twitchy. I jumped as an older man turned the page of his newspaper.

"Believe it," I said.

Great, that sounded bitchy. I pinched the bridge of my nose, wincing at a growing headache and took a deep breath. I didn't mean to take my frustrations out on Katie. Her babbling was annoying, but it wasn't really her fault. We were all worried. Katie just showed her emotions more than the rest of us.

And if Yuki had worn her feelings on her sleeve like Katie, we probably wouldn't be in this mess right now.

"Look, Yuki's gone AWOL and the Grabber's probably in town, but that doesn't mean she's in trouble," I said. I ignored my racing pulse and forced a smile. "She's probably hanging out in one of the study cubicles with her iPod and a stack of books."

"You really think so?" Katie asked.

"I know so," I said, sounding more confident than I felt. "We're just dotting our I's and crossing our T's. It's good to know where your friends are, especially when there's trouble in town."

Gordy nodded in agreement, or approval. He had been trying to comfort Katie by remaining calm, but I saw his mask slip when a petite girl dressed all in black rounded the corner.

Gordy started forward, raising his hand to get her attention, but when she lowered her stack of books onto a low rolling cart, the almond-shaped eyes and small mouth weren't Yuki's and her petite feet were strapped into shiny red sandals, not boots. Gordy's face fell and the color drained from his lips.

He reached up to smooth his asymmetrical bangs, covering his disappointment, but I'd seen the frightened face behind his calm exterior. Gordy was trying to hold it together, for Katie's sake, but underneath that cool façade was a guy in turmoil. Gordy had come to the same conclusion that I had—Yuki had a knack for trouble, and her disappearance had tragic outcome written all over it.

"That's Rin from my history class," I said. "I'll go ask if she's seen Yuki."

"Okay," Gordy said around a mouthful of hair.

He was chewing his bangs again.

"OhmygoshIcan'tbelieveshe'sreallymissing," Katie said.

Katie reached for Gordy with a shaking hand and he put his arm around her, pulling her close. I felt a pang of jealousy. I wished that Simon could be here right now, but we needed his tracking skills to find Yuki. I hoped that he was having more luck in his search than the three of us.

I was beginning to suspect that Yuki wasn't here in the safety of the library. But if she wasn't here, then where could she be?

I didn't like the answers my brain conjured in reply.

Chapter 24
Calvin

The west side of town turned up nothing. I wasn't as skilled at tracking as Simon, but I could often feel Yuki through our bond. So far I sensed nothing.

I tried to take that as a good sign.

If Yuki was in trouble, I'd know it, right? I sure hoped that was true. Yuki had mentioned feeling a strange tingling beneath the skin, where her spirit tattoo twines around her ankle, when we needed each other in the past. I rubbed my arm, but my tattoo felt normal.

I also tried reaching out to Yuki with my wolf spirit, but the search was fruitless. No matter how hard I concentrated, I couldn't sense Yuki's presence. Was she too far away, or had our bond grown weak?

Simon's words returned to me, as they had numerous times since our argument. Was I really bad for Yuki?

I drove slowly past the flea market on Elm Street, but couldn't feel Yuki's presence. Last autumn, I found the perfect gift for Yuki in one of these market stalls. Amidst disembodied doll heads, Beatles memorabilia, and old issues of TV Guide, an antique compass had lain buried.

I had been shopping with Yuki. She'd dragged me to the flea market after sitting through a chakra clearing workshop I'd wanted to attend. She said that shopping was my penance for making her tap her face for hours—which was, of course, an exaggeration. But I tagged along anyway.

I didn't share Yuki's love of retro lunch boxes and vintage clothing, but I dug through the detritus of people's lives alongside her. I was looking for a small trinket to appease her, but found something more romantic instead.

We had been dating for nearly a month and I had been searching for a special gift to mark our one month anniversary. The compass was perfect. It had brass knobs and screws. I thought Yuki would like the steampunk look of it and the fact that it was a compass gave me an idea. I waited until the following day and gave it to her with a note that read, "so that you may always find your way back to me." I had wondered if my note was too sappy, but Yuki has kept the compass with her ever since.

Gazing out the truck window as the flea market passed by, I had to wonder if Yuki would ever find her way back to me…or if it was already too late.

Chapter 25
Yuki

I sat upright, giving myself a dizzying head rush, as something brushed against my face. I spied a tall cluster of switchgrass waving in the air beside me and let out the breath I was holding. In my dream, the spindly grass that touched my face had been replaced by skeletal fingers. I was relieved to be rid of nightmare monsters, but where had the tall grass come from?

And when had I fallen asleep?

I looked around and frowned. I sat in a patch of dry grass that whispered as it swung to and fro in the warm breeze. The light wind made my hair dance around my head, tickling the back of my neck. Unable to see over the giant vegetation, I dusted off my skirt and rose to my feet.

"Oh," I said, my words lost on a gust of wind.

I was standing in the dream world that exists between the human realm and the ever-after, where spirits of the dead reside. Well, most spirits reside there. Some souls become trapped on earth if they are the unfortunate victim of tragic death or have unfinished business. That's where I come in. With my ability to smell the dead, I help to locate and communicate with those spirits trapped on my plane of existence and lead them to the light.

Of course, it's never that easy. That part about unfinished business? Yeah, most ghosts are pretty insistent about wrapping up those loose ends before departing my world.

Like the ghost who smelled like roses, lanolin, and dark room chemicals.

In fact, if I am here in the dream realm, then that means my body is asleep back in the real world. The thought of my body slumped over my painting stool, helpless, on that remote stretch of park trail, gave me the creeps. It would be getting dark soon, if night hadn't fallen already, and my body was alone in the woods with only a strange ghost for company.

I needed to find out why I'd been brought here, so I could get back to my body.

Usually when I appear in this place, my dung beetle spirit guide is nearby. I spun in a slow circle, searching for my guide.

"Where are you?" I muttered.

"I am here, child," a rasping voice echoed in my head.

I felt something move behind my back and turned to see my spirit guide looming over me. I have no idea where a seven foot tall dung beetle could have been hiding. *I probably didn't want to know.*

"Um, hi," I said lamely. "Is everything okay?" I hadn't tried to summon my spirit guide, and had, in fact, been working with a ghost before I appeared in this place. What other reason could explain this meeting? Had something terrible happened? "Wait. Is Cal hurt?"

I struggled to remain calm, but Cal had nearly died from a head injury a few months ago and his spirit had ended up here. Was that why I was summoned? Had Cal been in an accident?

I felt like a frightened bird was caged in my chest.

I had been in such a hurry to begin work on my painting today after school that I'd jumped out of Cal's truck without even asking where he was going. There were plenty of dangerous roads around Wakefield.

"Hush, child, your wolf is safe and sound in the human realm," she said.

"Oh, okay," I said, taking a deep breath. "Then why am I here?"

"I have a message for you," she said. *"As you know child, scarabs bury their eggs in the ground, but some humans dig into the soil of Mother Earth for other purposes. An evil man has hidden his secrets in the ground."*

"So, I, like, need to dig a hole or something?" I asked. I bit my lip, feeling totally confused. Why did my spirit guide always have to speak in riddles?

"The answers you seek are beneath the earth," she said.

My spirit guide lifted her arms above her head in a series of bizarre motions, as if she were directing a plane to land. The wind picked up and lifted dry sand and red dust into mini-tornados all around me. I closed my eyes and slapped a hand over my face to cover my nose and mouth.

"Don't forget child," she said. *"The answers are there for you to discover, if you take the time to look."*

*****

I woke with a gasp, returning to my body where it sat sprawled over the small stool. I sat upright and stretched, feeling stiff and sore. I shook the pins and needles sensation out of my foot and looked myself over. The front of my clothes felt damp, but it hadn't rained while my spirit was away. *Son of dung beetle, rain would have ruined my painting.*

I stood, checking for damage. My painting sat safely on its easel, but I couldn't say the same for my clothes.

Paint covered my chest where I'd slouched over the palette, and more shone wetly across my lap. *Great, that's never coming out.*

I grabbed a rag and wiped away some of the paint, but gave up. My clothes would just have to wait. It was getting dark, fast. I started packing up my things, careful to secure my new painting on the back of the bicycle where nothing would touch the drying paint. I'd have to be careful while riding home in the dim light. One spill on my bike would totally destroy the work I completed today.

The sun was already setting, reminding me of the need to leave and the fact that I had missed my dinner. My stomach growled its displeasure.

I searched quickly through my backpack and retrieved a bag of trail mix, skittles, and bottled water. I gulped water and ate a few mouthfuls of trail mix. The ghost continued to hover beside the rose bush, making me suddenly feel guilty about not sharing my food. But ghosts can't eat, right?

Still it seemed rude not to share.

I approached the ghost with a handful of trail mix, trying to figure out where to leave the offering. A sun bleached rock peeked out of the ground beneath the rose bush, presenting an unlikely place to dine, but it was better than placing the food in a patch of grass.

I knelt, not caring about my already ruined skirt, and brushed off the rock with my hand. Rain and wind had uncovered some of the stone, but as I touched the dirt, clumps of soil and moss fell away in clumps.

My spirit guide was right—there really was something buried beneath the ground.

And, unless it was just my imagination, this wasn't a rock. I'd found a dead body. I dropped the food to the ground, suddenly not feeling so hungry.

Oh em gees, I just touched a dead person. I wiped my hand down my skirt and tried to stifle a scream that rose up from my toes to my mouth. I swallowed the scream, but my stomach churned loudly. I was seriously regretting eating that trail mix.

I squinted in the growing dark. I've watched a lot of horror movies and knew in my gut what I was looking at. *Oh yeah, that's a human skull alright.*

The twilit skull seemed to draw the final glow of light from the fading day, casting the accusing eye sockets into shadow. Even the overhanging rose bush, which had looked so beautiful a few moments ago, now seemed to reach its thorns ominously above my head.

I crawled backward, distancing myself from the ghoulish find. Strands of hair had fallen loose and now hit my shoulders as I shook my head in denial.

"No, no, no," I whispered. "I didn't just spend the day with a dead body."

Ghosts are spooky enough, but some poor person's skull?—that was just plain freaky. I need to get out of here, now.

I looked around making sure everything I had brought with me was strapped securely to my bike. I was painfully aware of how alone I was here, just me and the ghost of the person buried beneath my feet.

I dug my cell phone out of my backpack and speed-dialed Cal. My call went straight to voicemail. It seemed like an eternity before the phone beeped, allowing me to leave a message.

"Cal, please call me back" I said, voice going shrill. "I'm near the park, on some freaky old trail and...I, I found a ghost and its b-b-body."

I hung up feeling lightheaded. Talking about the skeleton only made my fear worse. I needed to hear a person's voice—someone alive—and I wanted someone to know where I was.

I hit the second speed-dial on my phone.

Chapter 26
Emma

I was exiting the library with Gordy and Katie, when my phone started to vibrate. I'd turned the ringer off while inside, but left it on vibrate so I wouldn't miss a call or text from Cal and Simon. Maybe they'd found Yuki.

But the picture on the phone wasn't Cal's smiling face or Simon's smoldering eyes. A ridiculous picture of Yuki, eating a waffle the size of her head, flashed on the screen. I hit accept and whipped the phone to my ear so fast, I nearly punch myself in the face.

"Yuki?" I asked.

Gordy and Katie looked at me excitedly. If Yuki was calling, then maybe she was okay.

"Emma, I know w-w-we're not really sp-p-peaking right now, but I am so creeped out," Yuki said.

"Where are you?" I asked.

"S-s-some spooky old park trail," she said.

"Wakefield Park?" I asked.

"Yes," she said.

Yuki's voice sounded small and shaky. Why was she so scared? Was she hurt? Had she experimented with some crazy street drug? Was the Graduation Grabber there now?

And what was she doing in Wakefield Park?

"Are you okay?" I asked. "We've been looking all over town for you."

"I'm okay, but I found a ghost and…it led me to a skull out here in the woods," she said.

"You're out there now?" I asked. "With a dead body?"

"Um, yeah, a dead body and its ghost," she said wryly.

I wondered if I should tell her about the Grabber. Yuki was already frightened and if I told her that a serial killer who targeted teen girls was in town, she'd totally freak. But if I didn't tell her and some random guy showed up and offered his help, she might wander off with a murderer.

Someone would have to inform Yuki that the Graduation Grabber was back in town.

"Have you talked to Calvin?" I asked.

"No," she said. "His phone went straight to voicemail."

Great, I would have to be the one to tell her. If Calvin was tracking Yuki in his wolf form, he wouldn't have his phone with him. Maybe I could rig up some kind of hands-free, paws-free, phone on a collar for times like this, but that would have to wait. There were more important things to worry about.

"Not to freak you out or anything, but there's something I have to tell you," I said. "The reason we've all been looking for you is because a girl from our school went missing. The authorities think the Graduation Grabber has returned."

"Son of dung beetle," she muttered.

"How did you get out there anyway?" I asked.

I knew that Yuki hadn't received a ride from me, Simon, Calvin, Gordy, or Katie. But it was a long walk from Yuki's house to the park. Had she taken a bus part of the way? Or hitched a ride?

Goosebumps sprouted across the back of my neck at the thought of Yuki getting into a car with a stranger, especially with the Grabber lurking around looking for his second victim.

"I rode my bike," she said. I let out a relieved sigh. At least she hadn't been hitchhiking. "And, um, Emma? It's getting really dark out here. I think I need to start riding back toward town."

"Okay, can you keep your phone on?" I asked.

"Yeah, I think so," she said. "The battery looks like it has a full charge."

"Good, put your phone in your bag, or a pocket, and start riding toward the park entrance," I said. "We'll meet you there."

"Thanks Emma," she said.

"Any time," I said.

And I meant it. Yuki was my best friend. Our recent fighting seemed foolish now that she was in danger. When we got through all of this, we were due for a long talk and lots of soy ice cream.

The phone grew muffled and quiet as Yuki tucked it away and started bicycling. I turned to Katie, who was waiting excitedly beside Gordy, and handed her the phone.

"Katie, keep that line open," I said. "And please try to keep listening in case Yuki tries to tell us something. I need my hands free to drive."

I grabbed my keys, but Gordy put his hand on my arm stopping me from rushing to my car.

"Wait, is Yuki in trouble?" he asked.

"I don't know," I said. "I hope not. But she found a human skull out in a remote section of Wakefield Park and she's pretty freaked out."

"Eep!" Katie squeaked.

"I promised Yuki that we'd drive out to the park entrance and meet her there," I said.

Gordy stepped back and I raced down the stone library steps, with Gordy and Katie struggling to keep up. Katie put my phone to her ear as she ran and gave me a thumbs-up. Apparently the phone was working and there were no signs of trouble.

We all piled into my car and I took a deep breath. Yuki better be okay. Night was falling and there was no telling what creepy things were out in those woods.

I was struck with a terrible thought.

What if the body Yuki found belonged to one of the Grabber's victims? The police never found Rose Peterson. Yuki may have unwittingly discovered the site of one of the Grabber's body dumps. And if he'd used that location successfully before, what was to keep him from returning to the spot and using it again?

Chapter 27
Calvin

Driving to the outskirts of town turned up nothing. Every time I saw a flash of long dark hair or black clothing my heart would race, but it was never Yuki. There was no sign of Yuki anywhere. All of her usual haunts had been checked, now I was just clutching at smoke in a windstorm.

I turned west at Shaw's Creek, truck bouncing as I drove across the old covered bridge. As soon as I crossed to the opposite embankment, my arm started itching like fire ants marched beneath the skin.

For the first time since Emma's phone call, I smiled. Yuki and I had matching tattoos, hers was on her ankle, but my tattoo was on my arm—right where the itching and tingling had begun. Our tattoos were more than a symbol of our love. They were evidence of the bond between werewolf mates.

The fact that Yuki wasn't a werewolf was unusual, but it didn't weaken our bond. Spirit ink, blended during a full moon, contained the essence of werewolf ancestors who chose to aid the chosen couple. Those spirits came to me now, causing the itching beneath the skin, strengthening my link to my mate.

Yuki must be nearby.

I used the first designated pull over, an empty picnic spot, to move my truck off the narrow road. I stopped scratching at my arm and closed my eyes, reaching out with my wolf spirit. Setting my hands on my thighs, palms facing upward, I breathed in deeply through my nose and out through my mouth.

My wolf spirit seemed eager to heed my call, and with a nod in my mind's eye, leapt to meet my request. In spirit form my wolf has no physical substance and could run, literally, through the forest, unimpeded by trees and tangled undergrowth.

Just as I began to worry how far my wolf spirit could travel from my body, it stopped in its tracks.

There.

It was faint, but I could sense Yuki's presence to the North West. That was strange, even for Yuki. There's not much out in that direction and, without a car, it was a long hike from town.

I growled as a flash of panic ran down through our bond. Yuki was in trouble.

I jumped out of the truck and stashed the keys beneath the wheel-well. Listening for approaching vehicles, I took one last look around the picnic area. With no humans in sight, I ran for the woods.

I needed to reach Yuki, and the fastest way to do that was to track her while in my wolf form. I hoped that we were close enough to Yuki's location. Now that my wolf had identified Yuki through our spirit link, I should be able to pick up her scent. But I was still learning my wolf skills. Hopefully the lessons Simon had given me would pay off.

Quickly removing my clothes, I wound them into a tight roll and tied them around my waist. If I had to travel far, they wouldn't emerge unscathed, but bringing my clothing with me could save time if I had to change back to human form. My sneakers and phone I left behind. They would be too cumbersome tied against my body and I wasn't going to carry them in my mouth.

With my clothing secured, I started to run.

I began shifting into wolf form, branches hit my face as I ran. The transformation wasn't painful, but once my arms and legs began to shift, I had to stop running. Crouching on matted leaves and pine spills, I felt my awareness expand. The forest suddenly seemed so alive—squirrels chattering, birds singing, rodents burrowing—that I felt dizzy. I shook my head against the overwhelming cacophony of sounds.

My teeth lengthened, becoming fangs, and fingers rapidly transformed into claws. I blinked as the forest, so deafening mere seconds before, went quiet. The birds had gone silent in their trees and animals seeking refuge hid beneath the ground or stood frozen in place, waiting for the predator to pass.

My transformation was complete.

I tilted my head, sniffing loudly and tasting the air with my tongue. Yuki hadn't come this way, but she was close.

I turned and took a step forward. There. It was faint, but the trail led deeper into the woods.

I ran.

More panic ran through the bond and I struggled not to howl. I didn't want to give up my position until I knew what dangers Yuki faced. If keeping my presence secret would give the girl I loved an advantage, then I would become one with the lengthening shadows that filled the forest.

I would become one with the night.

Chapter 28
Yuki

My phone rested safely inside my backpack while I pedaled like flying monkeys were hot on my tail. Knowing that my friends were there with me, on the phone, gave me strength. Having Emma included as one of those friends brought tears to my eyes. Thankfully the rush of wind in my face dried the tears before they could fall.

Speaking of falling, it was a miracle that I hadn't wrecked my bike or flown over the handle bars. Night had truly come to Wakefield Park in all its lightless glory. Tree roots and rocks littered the narrow trail and branches snaked out to touch my face and tangle in my hair.

The only reason I hadn't fallen off my bike was the appearance of two glowing ghosts in my path. Well, that and the white knuckled grip I had on my handlebars.

Jackson had emerged from the gloom, responding to my fear. As an ethereal creature there was little he could do to help, but he did find one task he could tackle. Jackson joined Rose a few yards ahead of me, lighting the trail and keeping me from accidentally wrapping my bicycle around a tree.

So I rode as fast as I could. My legs burned as I pedaled like mad, following the two flitting ghosts who had become shining beacons against the night.

Sweat ran into my face and blood pounded in my ears. If I survived this night, I was totally taking up exercise. Maybe I'd even join Cal on one of his trips to Wolf Camp. The werewolves there were always engaging in outdoor activity. You could say that it ran in their blood—it certainly didn't run in mine.

Cal went to Wolf Camp monthly. I'd been there once, when we went to ask Simon for help, but hadn't returned. As alpha it was Cal's duty to make an appearance before his people.

Maybe this month I would join Cal at his side. It was time I met the rest of his pack.

Jackson's vinegar smell and Rose's floral scent strengthened, jolting me from my thoughts. The strong smell impressions were my only warning before something, or someone, lumbered into sight.

I hit the handbrakes and stopped so fast that I bit my tongue. But I barely noticed the salty taste of blood filling my mouth.

A wolf stood in the center of the trail, blocking my way.

Chapter 29
Calvin

I could feel Yuki through our bond. With my enhanced wolf hearing, I could also hear heavy breathing and something crashing through the woods up ahead. She was close. But was she alright?

I rushed silently between the trees, moving so fast and stealthily that I was like a falcon flying through the dark forest. Reaching Yuki's side was my priority, but I was also on the hunt. Whatever danger Yuki faced, she wouldn't face alone.

Nearly there…

I burst out onto a narrow hiking trail as something came rushing toward me. It was Yuki, riding a bicycle. Yuki on a bicycle was peculiar, but my brain didn't have time to wonder at what she was doing. I could smell blood as she stopped on the trail before me.

And her clothing was drenched in something red and wet.

No, no, no, no…

Against my will, I let out a howl of pain and heartache. I was too late.

Wasn't I?

"Cal?" Yuki asked breathlessly.

I lowered my head, meeting her worried gaze.

"It really is you," she said. Yuki set her kickstand and, in a rush of black skirts and tousled hair, she wrapped herself around me. "You scared me half to death. I thought you were a wild animal, or the Grabber."

I snuffled over the surface of her clothes confused. I had smelled the tang of blood, but the wet, red substance that covered Yuki's skin and clothes wasn't blood after all. She was covered in paint.

Yuki lifted her head from my shoulder to stare into my eyes. Human eyes in a wolf's face, she'd told me once.

"Cal, we have to get out of here," she said. "Emma is on the phone and she said the Graduation Grabber is in Harborsmouth. She said there's already one girl missing, someone from our school, and…I found a person's skull back there."

She pointed to the trail behind her. As she talked, the smell of blood increased. I sniffed her face and she smiled giving me a kiss on the nose.

Yuki was definitely bleeding, and it was coming from her mouth.

I felt the fur begin rise in a ridge along my back. Yuki was my mate and I was bound to protect her. Adrenaline rushed through me and I tensed, ready to fight.

I was angry, but I was also worried. My tail tucked between my legs and I let out a whine. Yuki may be my mate, but she was human. She didn't have the advantage of werewolf healing that I had. She needed to get the injury in her mouth checked out.

And I had to find a way to protect her from the Grabber.

While the Graduation Grabber was on the loose, no teenage girl was safe. According to the police, the Grabber always abducted and killed two girls during the week before graduation. With one girl already missing, a second abduction was imminent. It was the Grabber's pattern—a pattern that put my friends and my mate at risk.

Yuki said that she had found a human skull nearby. If the skull belonged to one of the Grabber's victims, that discovery could put Yuki in even greater danger.

"Cal, hey, you listening?" she asked. "I said we need to get out of here. Emma, Gordy, and Katie are going to meet us down at the front gates." She pointed downhill. "We have to get out of the park."

I nodded, backing up a step. She was right. We needed to get out of these woods, where a killer might be lurking. When Yuki was safe from harm, I could return with Simon to examine the skull that she had found.

I took point, wondering for the first time how Yuki could see anything at all. She didn't have wolf eyesight, but was getting on her bike without stumbling. I was sure there was an interesting story there, but it could wait.

Leading the way, with Yuki riding behind me, I trotted down the trail. I stayed alert for any sight, sound, or smell that may indicate an approaching danger, but the most threatening thing I sensed was a bat searching for a hearty dinner of moths and mosquitoes. A bat could have caused a problem if it became tangled in Yuki's hair, but it flew away without her ever knowing it was there.

I loped ahead, checking around the next bend in the trail, and caught sight of artificial light. After the darkness of the woods the light hurt my eyes, making them water. I blinked against welling tears until I was certain of what I was seeing.

We had found the park gates.

Chapter 30
Simon

*H*orns blared as I ran across the highway. Playing chicken with human drivers may be foolish, but this was the fastest way to complete my search.

Plus, there's nothing like a near death experience to get your blood pumping. No wonder our dog cousins chased cars—it was invigorating.

Unfortunately, my search for Yuki was far less exciting. I had hoped to catch Yuki's scent by shifting into wolf form, but hadn't found any sign of her so far.

I sniffed the game trail running alongside the busy road, scenting deer and fox, but no Yuki. I had run out places to search. Should I circle back to my motorcycle and shift into my human form?

Cal had designated the east side of town as my search area, saying that he would look for Yuki to the west. Had Cal turned up anything while hunting the other side of town?

Being out of phone contact was becoming difficult. I had only been in wolf form for about an hour, but not knowing if Emma was still safe was eating me up inside. If I returned for my things, I could get a status update from Cal and check in with Emma.

It would be better than running around here in circles, chasing my tail. My tracking skills were heightened while in wolf form, but the east side of town was too populated to run around freely. I had already taken too many chances. If I didn't change back soon, someone was likely to call animal control, or take matters into their own hands.

I turned to the field behind me and started running back to my motorcycle. I needed to retrieve my things and shift back to my human form. I'd stashed my clothing and cell phone in a fallen tree a few yards from my bike. At this speed, I could be there in ten minutes.

Panting, I ran. Emma was a phone call away. I just had to make it to my phone without an ignorant human shooting me, or hitting me with their car. Considering the way Americans drive, I'd take my chances against a bullet.

I turned further from the road and raced across the open field.

Chapter 31
Yuki

I lost sight of Cal as he rounded a corner up ahead. My heart started pounding in my chest and my hands started to sweat. Not only was that totally gross, but sweaty hands also made it difficult to hold onto the handlebars.

It was completely silly for me to freak out. I was perfectly safe. Cal was just checking the trail ahead. He hadn't abandoned me. I wasn't in danger.

So why was I having a massive panic attack?

I'd been getting those more and more frequently. *Like I needed another thing to make my life crazy.* Smelling ghosts, and now seeing their glowing aura, was bad enough, but hyperventilating and sweating was a major pain, and totally unattractive.

I pedaled around the bend in the trail and saw Cal waiting for me. My heart slowed and a cool breath of air rushed into my oxygen-starved lungs. *See, silly, he's still there. He wouldn't run off and leave you here all alone.*

Relief washed away the panic, leaving me lightheaded. I was seeing spots and it took a minute to realize that two of those glowing dots weren't the product of my mind.

Cal had found the park gates.

Lights shone atop stone pillars at either side of the park entrance and another pair of lights was moving toward them. A car was approaching from the direction of the parking lot, shining its headlights across the gates. Was it Emma, a random passerby, or the Grabber?

Only one way to find out.

Cal started down the trail with me riding close behind. I was anxious to get out of this place and out of my paint spattered clothes. I could feel paint stiffening my blouse and drying beneath my fingernails as I rode.

As I struggled to keep up with Cal, my tongue began to throb. It hadn't hurt when I first bit it, but now my tongue ached with every beat of my racing heart.

If the car at the gates belonged to Emma, I'd let her brew me up one of her noxious teas. Adrenaline had pushed away my pain, but now every part of me was beginning to hurt. My back and neck ached from my nap in the woods and a cramp was forming in my left leg. A headache was also creeping in behind my eyes, probably the result of being in close proximity to two smelly ghosts.

I pushed through the pain and exhaustion to follow Cal across the last stretch of park. When we neared the gates, we both stopped in the center of the trail. Cal came to stand in front of me, his back nearly the same height as my bike while in his wolf form. He made a formidable barrier between me and any danger.

I raised a paint covered hand to shield my eyes against the glare of headlights. The car was idling at the curb with its headlights aimed right at us. I couldn't see who was in the car. If it wasn't our friends, we were in trouble. There was no way Cal would pass for a dog.

Son of a dung beetle.

In my race to escape the park, and Cal's fierce effort to protect me, we'd made a mistake. Unless this car contained the Grabber, Cal will have exposed his true form for no reason. Even if the car was Emma's, Gordy and Katie would be waiting inside, and they didn't know Cal's secret.

They had no idea that werewolves existed.

Chapter 32
Emma

My friends raced toward us, heading for the park gates, Yuki on her bicycle and Calvin in his wolf form.

That was a problem.

What was I supposed to tell Gordy and Katie? "Oh look, there's Yuki and her pet wolf" just wasn't believable. Plus, Katie had been listening to Yuki through my phone. She'd heard Yuki talking to Calvin. So even if Katie and Gordy believed that the wolf was tame, how would I explain Calvin's sudden disappearance?

Of course, telling them that the wolf was in fact Calvin, that he was a werewolf, wasn't believable either. And most importantly, it wasn't my secret to share.

But what was I supposed to do?

Maybe if I got out and let Yuki and Calvin know who was shining high beams at their faces, Calvin could run off and change into human form. There'd be lots of questions, but we could deal with that later.

"You two stay in the car," I said. "I'm going to see if Yuki's alright."

"There's a w-w-wolf," Katie said.

"It's alright," I said. "I'm used to working with large animals. This is what I do all day. I'll be fine."

"Are you sure?" Gordy asked. His voice was a whisper for my ears only. He didn't want to question my judgment in front of Katie, but he was willing to come with me if needed backup.

I nodded. Reaching for the door handle, I swung my medical bag over my shoulder. I hoped that I wouldn't need it, but there was something on Yuki's clothes that looked suspiciously like blood.

Hopefully it was just a trick of the light.

I was better at treating animals than people, which was the reason the wolf pack elders were sending me to veterinary school, but I could patch up a human in a pinch. Walking toward Yuki, I figured this was one of those situations.

The clinical part of my brain began assessing injuries as she came closer. There was dried blood on Yuki's skirt, blouse, arms, face, and hands. Her pupils were constricted against the bright light, a good sign that she wasn't drugged—willingly or against her will. Thin red welts rose on the sides of her face and across her arms.

What had happened to my best friend?

"Hey," I said, nodding at Calvin and Yuki both.

"Hey," Yuki said.

Calvin's tongue lolled in a goofy wolf grin. Apparently, he was happy to see me. We were making progress.

"Calvin, if you don't want Katie and Gordy asking too many questions, go run off and change forms," I said. "They're in too much shock to think about it right now, but if you stick around they're going to want to know what a wild wolf is doing with Yuki. They're also going to start getting worried about where you are. Katie's been listening in on Yuki's phone and heard her talking to you."

"And they don't know about werewolves," Yuki said.

"Right," I said.

Calvin looked at Yuki, and for a moment I thought he wouldn't leave her side. Werewolf boys were some of the most stubborn, protective creatures on the planet.

I should know, since I was dating one myself.

"Go on," Yuki said. "Just come back really quick."

Sweat shone on her pale face, but Yuki held her head high and put her hands on her hips. It seemed to pain her to be separated from Calvin, but she could be just as selfless as he. She had made it clear before that she would never do anything to risk discovery of his secret.

Yuki was trying to protect him.

Calvin seemed to finally realize this and loped away. I closed the last few feet between us and took Yuki's hand.

"Where are you hurt?" she asked.

"I hurt all over," she said, shaking her head. "But I'm alright. "Just a bit tongue and some bumps and bruises…and one of my headaches."

"What about the blood?" I asked.

That much blood couldn't possibly have come from a cut on her tongue.

"Blood?" she asked.

Yuki looked down at herself and laughed.

"Oh, that's not blood," she said. "It's paint."

With no more worries of serious injury, I wrapped Yuki in a fierce hug.

"Don't ever do that again," I said.

"Do what?" she asked.

"Oh, I don't know," I said. "Fight with me, stop talking to me, scare me half to death…"

"Okay, okay, I promise," she said, smiling.

"Don't worry," Calvin said, walking up behind Yuki. "I'm not ever letting her out of my sight again. She won't have another chance to scare us all into thinking she's dead."

Seeing the wolf leave, and Cal appear, was Gordy and Katie's cue to get out of the car and join our little reunion. Gordy was chewing his hair and Katie fidgeted with the ties on her blouse.

"You guys thought I was dead?" she asked, smile fading.

"It's a long story," I said. "We can talk over pizza after we get you home and cleaned up."

"Okay," she said.

My phone rang, making everyone jump.

"Sorry," I said. I dug my phone out of my pocket and saw Simon's eyes flash on the screen. "It's Simon."

"Of course it's Simon," Yuki said. "We mentioned pizza."

Chapter 33
Yuki

After strapping my bike to Emma's car, my friends drove me home. I felt like I was in a daze. The entire trip was a blur, with little pit stops of clarity when each friend said goodbye.

We dropped Cal off at a picnic area where he'd left his truck. He kissed my forehead and promised to meet us for pizza later. He whispered something about needing to retrieve his shoes so he could go to the restaurant with us. It was only then that I realized he was barefoot. *Oh, right, wolves don't wear sneakers.*

Next we left Gordy and Katie at the pizza parlor. They went inside armed with a hefty pizza order. Apparently, worrying had made everyone ravenous.

My stomach growled at the scent of garlic and tomato sauce that filled the car as Gordy and Katie closed the door and Emma prepared to drive away. All I'd had to eat was that one handful of trail mix. Finding the skull had made me feel queasy, but now I was starving.

Usually it was smelly ghosts that ruined my appetite, now it was dead bodies—I was moving up in the world. *Lucky me.*

I wanted to know more about the skull in the woods, and my new smelly friend, but my friends came first. Emma brought me home and chatted with my parents about our upcoming graduation while I ran upstairs to shower and change into clothes that didn't look like they were spattered with blood. The "I'm the survivor of a zombie massacre" couture was kind of cool, but Emma assured me that our fellow diners at the pizza parlor wouldn't appreciate the look.

As usual, she was probably right.

I scrubbed myself pink. Paint had soaked through my clothes, leaving red circles on my skin that looked suspiciously like roses. The smell of roses permeating my bathroom added to the illusion. I poured more sandalwood scented shower gel onto the loofa and continued to scour my skin.

When the worst of the stains were removed, and the water running down the drain ran clear, I finally stepped out. There was no more delaying the inevitable. It was time to face my friends.

And the ghost waiting behind my bathroom door.

Chapter 34
Emma

Yuki sat so quietly in the passenger seat. It was almost like she wasn't there. For some reason, that made me sad.

I'd missed my friend these past few weeks. To finally have her back in my life, but not knowing what to say to her seemed terribly unfair. I had hoped that Yuki would be the first to talk, being the vivacious one and all, but as soon as we'd left her parents' house she had withdrawn into herself.

I snuck a glance over at Yuki and didn't like what I saw. She was sitting slumped in her seat, picking at ragged, paint stained fingernails.

"So, what were you painting?" I asked.

I needed to pry Yuki out of her shell. Talking about our recent fights over Simon, or her debilitating fear of the school supply closet, would only stress her out. I figured that bringing up the skull she'd discovered also fell into the "stress Yuki out" category. That left one topic—the mysterious painting strapped on the back of Yuki's bike.

Where had she been on her bicycle? What was so important that she had to paint it late in the evening? And why had she lied to Calvin about it?

"Huh?" Yuki said. "Oh, right, the painting. I guess you saw it on the back of my bike."

"Well, that and you were covered in paint," I said.

"It's for art class," she said. "There's this final project that I have to present next week, if I want to graduate. I kind of left it until the last minute."

Yuki tilted her head, shaking a curtain of dark hair down to cover her face. Was she embarrassed? I may be really into grades and school performance myself, but I'd never judge Yuki for slacking. Her procrastination just seemed to confirm my suspicions that she was suffering from PTSD. Finishing projects and looking ahead to the future were difficult tasks for someone who had recently faced life-changing fear. She didn't need to feel ashamed.

I just hoped her ability to graduate wasn't at risk.

Being kept back was bad enough, but I didn't want to think about how hard it would be for Yuki to face that school, and the location of her confinement, without any of her friends there for support. We wouldn't be there to protect her. Yuki would have to face her fears alone.

I'd have to look into Yuki's grades later, but now I was curious about this painting.

"So why did you tell Calvin you were staying home to study for exams?" I asked.

"Once it was graded, I wanted to give the painting to Cal…as a graduation present," she said, shrugging. "That's why I didn't tell him, and why I went somewhere outdoors to paint."

"Oh, right," I said. That made sense. "Calvin loves the woods, and the park. But why were you deep into the park trails?"

"Why else?" she said. "A smelly ghost led me there."

That sounded like a story that Simon and Calvin would also be interested in hearing. I pulled into a parking spot outside the pizza parlor deep in thought. After Gordy and Katie leave tonight, I was going to make Yuki spill about this ghost.

But first, it was time to eat.

Chapter 35
Calvin

The bell over the door jingled and Yuki and Emma walked into the restaurant. They've always been opposites, one blond and dressed all in white and the other dark haired and all in black, but tonight those differences went deeper than appearances.

Yuki cast furtive glances around the room, eyes never resting on one person for long before turning her gaze to the floor. Her sleeves were pulled down over her hands, shoulders hunched and black and hot pink hood pulled up, as if she were trying to hide inside her hoodie. When she sat in the empty chair beside me, she drew her booted feet up onto the chair rung and wrapped her skirt and arms around her legs like a cocoon.

Where was the Yuki that I knew? Would that vibrant butterfly ever emerge again?

After a worried glance at Yuki, Emma strode into the room making a beeline for Simon. Her eyes never left his face, as if they both communicated their entire day through that one look. Emma looked intense, confident, and...in love.

I was used to seeing those things in Yuki, but now she sat hunched beside me, her body language screaming "stay away, don't touch me, don't hurt me." I had involuntarily lifted my hand to reach for hers, but let it drop to my lap, thinking better of it. What would I do if she flinched away from me?

I didn't think I could handle that right now, not after Simon's biting words.

"Hey, Yuki," Gordy said. "I ordered you a loaded veggie pizza, extra cheese."

"Thanks Gordster," she said.

A tiny smile fluttered across her face, but all too soon it was gone. Like a frightened bird that smile wouldn't settle into place, choosing instead to fly away to safer ground, leaving Yuki staring blankly at the steaming slice of pizza on her plate.

"So, like, what was that wolf doing in the park?" Katie asked. "I mean, shouldn't we call animal control or something?"

I tried not to groan. Of course Katie would have remembered seeing me at the park in my wolf form. She may have been too startled, and focused on Yuki's safety, to say much at the time, but she had had an hour to sit here and wonder about it. Spotting a wolf this close to town was definitely strange. In fact, the only wolves around for miles were werewolves.

Our pack made sure to keep track of wolf activity, since a wolf sighting in the area could bring unwanted trouble to my people. And now I'd gone and risked discovery because I was too focused on protecting Yuki. The last thing my pack needed was animal control combing the woods, looking for wolves.

"Um, well, it didn't hurt me or anything," Yuki said.

"But wolves are wild animals," she said. "And it was huge. I think I would have died of fright if I saw that thing while walking at the park. Aren't they, like, dangerous?"

That thing? I liked Katie and knew she was more comfortable with her nose in a book than out wandering the wilderness, but her reaction to my wolf form stung. Yuki obviously needed saving, she just wasn't focused enough to keep up her side of the conversation, but my mind kept returning to Katie's comment like a tongue worrying at a sore tooth.

Thankfully Simon and Emma came to the rescue.

"Actually, love, wolves are quite harmless," Simon said. "It's humans you have to be wary of."

"Right, like the Graduation Grabber," Emma said.

"So what's all this about the Grabber anyway?" Yuki asked. "You said a girl went missing?"

"Yes, the Graduation Grabber, the worst serial killer to ever plague the streets of Wakefield, is back in town," Emma said.

Chapter 36
Yuki

I sighed with relief as Gordy and Katie said their goodbyes. Trying to answer their questions while keeping secrets made my head spin. But as soon as the restaurant door closed, all of the remaining eyes at the table turned to me. I fidgeted under the curious stares of my friends, knowing that they were all dying to know about the new ghost in my life.

But I was just dying to go home.

While I picked at my pizza, Emma had relayed the information she heard on the evening news report. I hoped my parents didn't catch the late night broadcast. They never would have let us go out for pizza if they'd known that a girl from my school had gone missing.

Gordy, Katie, Simon, and Cal all had stories to add to the conversation. We had all heard tales about the Graduation Grabber. He was the bogeyman of Wakefield, a monster who returned each year during graduation week to abduct and kill innocent teen girls—until four years ago when he seemed to disappear.

When the killings stopped, most Wakefield residents went on with their lives. The popular theory was that the Grabber had been arrested for murders elsewhere, and remained in prison. People said that he was dead, some even going so far as to speculate that the Grabber had been killed by his final victim, Rose Peterson.

Rose's body has never been found. But I had a nagging suspicion where it might be buried...and who my mysterious new ghost pal was.

Of course, I couldn't talk about ghosts and smell impressions while Katie and Gordy were having pizza with us. Now that they were gone, it was time to talk.

Instead, I dipped a piece of fried zucchini into a cup of tomato sauce and filled my mouth. Even though I'd been starving earlier, I hadn't eaten much of my pizza. I spent most of the evening trying not to jump at every sound. I clenched my teeth for so long, my jaw ached.

But I continued to take bites of the zucchini, delaying the questions I knew would come. I was so tired. I wanted to go home, crawl under the covers, and pretend that today hadn't happened. Too bad sleep is where the nightmares were always lurking.

Terrifying dreams of sweaty jock assailants and leering grins from the J-team were there every night now, every time I closed my eyes and fell asleep.

I put down the fried zucchini and pushed my plate away, the food turning to ash on my tongue. I swallowed hard and focused on the dull throb where I'd bit myself earlier, trying to ignore the fear that gripped my chest and twisted my stomach.

It was ironic, the fear. I dealt with ghosts and werewolves all the time, but a couple of football jocks had reduced me to a cringing girl fearful of her own shadow. I felt like such a wimp. I tried to sit up straight and take a deep breath, but dread still strangled my lungs in its vice-like grip.

I settled for nodding to my friends.

"I know this is hard," Emma said, keeping her voice low. "But we have to know. You said you found a body near one of the park trails, and that a smell impression led you there. Did you learn anything from the ghost?"

"Do you think it's the missing girl from your school?" Simon asked. "The one who just went missing? If so, her parents deserve to know she's gone. They're worried bloody sick about her."

"No, it's not Sarah Randall," I said. I took a sip of water and cleared my throat. "The body I found was just a skeleton. Just a skull really, I didn't dig any farther once I could tell it was human. But the person must have been buried there for quite awhile."

"What can you tell us?" Cal asked, giving me a weak smile. "We want to help."

I dropped my head onto my fist and stared at a congealing blob of cheese on my plate. There was no escaping their questions and worried looks, but where to begin?

"It's like I was saying to Gordy and Katie," I said. "I had an art project to finish, so I rode my bike to the park hoping to find a nice outdoor scene to paint. What I didn't tell them is that when I got there I was hit with a strong smell impression."

"What did it smell like?" Emma asked, leaning in across the table.

"It smelled, continues to smell, like roses, lanolin, and darkroom chemicals," I said. "But mostly, it smells like roses."

"And this ghost clung to you like you were its best mate, and led you to a human skull?" Simon asked.

"Yeah, something like that," I said. "I followed the ghost for a long time, until it stopped at a section of old broken wall. Growing up the wall was a huge climbing rose bush, so I took a break from riding and decided to paint the location. The roses were beautiful...I didn't know there was a dead body buried there."

Cal gave my free hand a quick squeeze, but I wasn't all that scared now. I had been afraid of someone trying to hurt me, like the J-team tried a few months ago, and how someone had possibly done to the body in the ground. The fear had lingered, but talking about it was helping.

The body in the woods had been buried in an unmarked grave in a secluded location. The ghost probably wanted a proper burial. If a murder had taken place, then someone needed to be brought to justice. And if the ghost had family, it may want them to know what really happened—why they had disappeared.

This ghost had unfinished business, and I was going to help it set things right.

"A ghost who smells like roses and was buried beneath a rose bush," Emma said. "Is it me, or does that sound like a possible match for Rose Peterson, the last girl to go missing before the Grabber disappeared?"

"They never found her body," Cal said. "It could be her."

The smell of pizza was immediately replaced by the strong scent of roses. I grabbed my head in both hands and bit my lip. *Oh yeah, I think we have a winner.*

"Are you alright?" Cal asked, placing his hand on my back. "You just went really pale."

"How can you tell?" Simon asked, raising one eyebrow.

"Har, har, har, very funny Simon," I said, wincing. "Well if the staggering smell impression and mind sucking headache is any indication, I'd say we've found Rose Peterson."

The ghost backed off, giving me room to breathe. She hadn't gone far. In fact, Rose hadn't left my side since we met at the park. She would give me space, but this ghost wasn't leaving—not until I discovered what unfinished business she had in our world.

Great, just what I needed. I had one week to pass my exams and graduate high school. Now I also had a ghost to babysit and a mystery to solve—all while a serial killer lurked in the shadows waiting for his second victim.

But for the first time in weeks, I was beginning to move forward. The tendrils of fear that tied me up inside retreated. I finally felt like my old self. I sat up straight and placed my booted feet on the floor.

It was time to help a ghost with its final wishes, and add a new member to my army of the dead.

Chapter 37
Emma

Yuki stopped slouching like she was trying to implode and a smile slid across her face. She met my gaze across the table with a steely glint in her eye.

"Let's go find out what this ghost really wants," she said.

Yuki reached out with her fist and we bumped knuckles across the table. I finally had my friend back.

But I knew she still needed help. You can't cure PTSD with pizza, though Yuki would argue that fact—she thought pizza cured everything. No, the ghost of Rose Peterson was a temporary distraction. I still had a lot to discuss with Yuki, but that conversation would have to wait. *Relax, ssshe'll be fine.*

I took the advice of the sibilant voice in my head and tried to focus on the task at hand. I had to admit that the mystery surrounding Yuki's new ghost pal was intriguing. I've assisted Yuki in the past on her mission to help spirits of the dead find peace, but the discovery of this ghost's remains, and the connection to the Graduation Grabber, brought this case home to roost.

Poor Rose Peterson.

I hadn't known Rose, I was in middle-school when she went missing, but I could easily identify with her. Rose was the age I am now, when the Grabber took her. We went to the same school, had the same teachers, walked the same halls, and lived in the same town. And now it was graduation week, the same time of year when she had been abducted.

Rose never had a chance to graduate, or grow old, but we could give her one thing. We could help bring her killer to justice.

We could prevent the Graduation Grabber from killing again.

"We need to find the Grabber before he kills Sarah Randall," I said.

Simon and Calvin nodded their agreement, but Yuki sucked in a breath and grabbed her head between paint stained hands.

"I think…" Yuki said. "I think that Rose would like that."

"Good," I said. "Then we need a plan. But first, let me order some hot water and I'll brew you up some tea for that headache."

"Okay," she said, turning green.

"Emma, love, do you have to do that here?" Simon asked, gesturing to the other diners. "I'm sure some of these people would like to enjoy the rest of their meal without smelling one of your concoctions."

"Why don't we head over to the cabin," Calvin said. "It will be easier to make our plans there and we can open the windows while you brew the tea."

"Good idea, mate," Simon said. "I was getting sick of whispering."

"Can we order more pizza to go?" Yuki asked. An impish grin slid across her face. "I'll need something to wash Emma's tea down with."

I rolled my eyes, but agreed. Yuki finally had her appetite back. That was a very good sign. My friend may not recover overnight, but together we could solve this mystery and help put back the pieces of Yuki's life.

If that took a massive order of udderly disgusting cheese covered pizza, so be it.

Chapter 38
Simon

I buried my face in another box of meat lover's pizza, trying to avoid the smell of Emma's teas, tinctures, and tisanes. I shook my head against the sharp herbal tang and wet hay scents that wafted in to mix with the delicious smell of beef and pork. I pinched my nose and shoved a slice of pizza into my mouth.

Werewolf heightened senses could be a sodding pain.

"That's disgusting," Yuki said.

The girl had a smile on her face for the first time in weeks, so I didn't bother to argue—just snorted my disdain, which led to a fit of choking and coughing. That sent Yuki into fits of laughter, until Emma shoved a mug of steaming medicinal tea into her hand.

Joke's on you, love. Now who's laughing?

I've had the displeasure of tasting Emma's herbal remedies before. They tended to taste like old leaves mixed with squirrel droppings, but don't ask me how I know that. I'm a wolf, I just do.

Calvin stood hip to hip with Yuki and gave her a sympathetic smile and a squeeze on the shoulder. I don't know how he tolerated standing so close to the noxious brew in Yuki's hand. Glad I wouldn't be kissing that later. There was no mouthwash on the planet that could combat Emma's herbal cures. Calvin was going to taste wet leaves and rodent droppings for a week. I snickered and started to choke again on a slice of pepperoni.

You'd think I'd learn.

"Here," Emma said, waving an amber bottle in my face. "Place a drop of this under your tongue. It will cure that cough."

I rushed backward so fast, I shattered a lamp and the milk crate it was resting on.

"Dude, that was my nightstand," Calvin said.

"Yes, very ghetto chic," I said. "I'll be sure to replace it tomorrow. I'm sure I can find something comparable at the town dump, or one of the alleys I was searching earlier today."

"Fine," Calvin said, running a hand through messy hair. That kid should really think about a professional haircut. "Just remember, you live here too. If you bring home something that reeks of urine and rotting garbage, we all suffer."

He had a point.

"You sound fine now," Emma said. She cocked her head, giving me a critical look over. "No more cough?"

"Yes, love," I said. "Cured by your ethereal beauty. No medicine necessary."

"I've died and gone to Hell," Yuki said, muttering into her cup.

"At least you don't have to live with him," Calvin said.

"You're no picnic, mate," I said. "You snore."

"It's true," Yuki said. "One time, I thought zombie bears had come to eat our brains, but it was just Cal taking a nap."

"Hey!" Calvin said.

"I have a remedy for snoring…" Emma said.

"No," we all said in unison.

Yuki giggled and Cal shook his head and slapped a hand over his mouth in mock horror.

"Fine, then let's get on with our planning," Emma said. "We have a girl to save and a ghost to lay to rest."

Chapter 39
Yuki

*I*t was nice being back in the cabin with my closest friends. Even having Simon around wasn't so bad. Maybe I had been too quick to judge Emma's choice of boyfriend. The two looked happy together.

Even if he was an old geezer.

The most surprising thing was that Simon, a total playboy, wasn't bragging about his exploits with other women. It was obvious that he only had eyes for Emma. The guy was completely in orbit around her.

Of course, that didn't mean that Simon wasn't a total pain in my butt. He was the most annoying werewolf on the planet, but he was Emma's werewolf. I was just going to have to get my head around that.

"I still think we need to focus on the smell impressions," I said. "The different scents always mean something significant."

"You think the smells could be clues to the ghost's identity and lead us to the killer?" Cal asked.

"Yeah," I said.

"Only you lot would follow a ghostly trail of smelly breadcrumbs," Simon said, shaking his head. "I still think we need to watch that burial site. The Grabber may return."

"What if we do both?" Emma said. "Calvin, can you ask someone from your pack to watch the place where Yuki found the skull?"

Cal looked thoughtful, then nodded.

"Yes, I'll call now," he said. "I also need to put a warning out on the network about a potential killer being in town. The Grabber may not be targeting werewolves, but my people need to be prepared."

"Aye, I'll fire up the computer and post a warning message," Simon said.

Cal pulled his phone from his pocket, while Simon busied himself with the old PC in the corner.

We had learned the hard way that a phone and email messaging system was crucial to pack safety. In the past, werewolf leaders had preferred secrecy rather than keeping an open line of communication within the pack. When a psychotic killer who hated werewolves went on a violent rampage, there was no system in place for contacting members of the pack who may be in danger.

Together we researched member identities, made a list of contact information, created emergency protocols, formed a call circle, and designed a computer program for sending messages electronically to all pack members. Cal had only been pack alpha for less than a year, but he was already making improvements to ensure the survival of his pack.

Cal was gravely serious about his responsibility as pack alpha. Ever since we were kids, he'd been the deep thinking philosophical one. When Cal set his mind to something, he didn't quit. Now his pack duties dominated much of his time, but he never shirked his duties. It was one of the many things about Cal that I found attractive.

I realized that I was staring at something else I found attractive about Cal, and blushed. There should be a law about looking that good in a pair of jeans. Turning to Emma, I lifted my empty mug in salute.

"Thanks for the tea," I said.

"Hey," Emma said.

"Yeah?" I asked.

"I just want you to know that you can talk to me, about anything," she said. "Any time, okay?"

Emma reached out and gave me an awkward hug, crushing the mug against my chest.

"Okay," I said.

That was weird. Maybe she was feeling guilty about our recent fighting? If so, she should relax. Most of our arguments were my fault. I had a short fuse lately, and Emma had been an easy target.

"Um, Emma?" I said. "Sorry about, you know, being so angry about Simon. He may be an old geezer, but you seem happy."

"I heard that," Simon said.

Pesky werewolf hearing.

Simon kept his back to me, focusing on the computer in front of him, but he didn't go rigid or stop working. I was ninety percent positive that he wasn't about to throw something in my direction. But I took a step to my left, placing myself behind Emma, just to be sure.

"We're okay," Emma said. "But if I find out you're flunking out this semester, I'll be extremely unhappy."

Emma's narrowed eyes tracked me as I moved to the other side of the room. Suddenly the cabin felt too small for the four of us.

Was it me, or were Emma and Simon a scary couple? They could make me run and hide without even twitching.

I found solace in Cal's presence. I don't know if it's a soul mate thing, or just a Cal thing, but I always felt better when he was close.

I leaned on the arm of the couch where Cal sat talking to a worried pack member. His calm voice was soothing and I tilted my head to rest on his shoulder. The deep vibration of his voice vibrated up through my cheek and made me smile.

Enjoying the relaxing moment while it lasted, I let my eyes unfocus and allowed my mind to wander. I could smell roses over the scent of wet dog rising from Cal.

Roses, lanolin, and dark room chemicals.

The tang of chemicals always made my nose wrinkle whenever I had to work in the school darkroom. But there was something magical about images rising from the toxic liquid, faces appearing beneath the red glow of the work lamp. With school almost over, I'd probably never step inside a darkroom again. As far as hobbies go, I preferred charcoals and paints over film.

But some people do use darkrooms after high school. Professional photographers continue to work with those chemicals every day.

And the school hires professionals to photograph our graduation ceremony each year.

Chapter 40
Calvin

"Oh em gees," Yuki said.

Yuki lifted her head from my shoulder so quickly that her hair flew up to tickle my face. I lifted an eyebrow in question and she flapped her hands at me to hurry and get off the phone.

The hysterical werewolf I'd been talking to was calm now and ready to call her teenage daughter to enforce a curfew until the Grabber was caught. I assured her that she could call me any time and hung up.

Yuki's eyes were open so wide she looked like a startled owl, but a smile was creeping onto her pale face as she bounced on the arm of the couch.

"What happened?" I asked.

"Yes, do tell," Simon said, spinning his chair toward us.

"I know that look," Emma said, resting a hand on Simon's shoulder and smiling at Yuki. "Girl, you figured something out, right?"

"Yeah, I think I did," Yuki said. "Remember how I said that the ghost smells like roses? Well it also smells like lanolin and darkroom chemicals. And I was thinking…if it's a clue to the killer's identity, then who would smell like darkroom chemicals…and visit Wakefield during graduation week?"

"The school, even some of the students' families, hire professional photographers to photograph the graduation ceremony," I said.

"It's also wedding season," Emma said. I raised an eyebrow at her and she blushed all the way to the roots of her pale blond hair. "Well it is, and that means photographers in the area. In fact, the second most popular location for weddings around here, besides the beach, is the park."

"Where Yuki found the body," I said.

"The Graduation Grabber could totally be a photographer," Yuki said. "We may be one step closer to discovering his identity."

"And to saving Sarah Randall," I said.

"Oh em gees, indeed," Simon said.

He sounded impressed. It was about time. I knew that it took a lot to earn Simon's respect, but Yuki's paranormal abilities and problem solving skills may have finally burrowed through his thick skull.

I let out a deep breath and leaned back in my chair. I finally had my pack returned to me.

The past few months had been torture. I tried not to let on just how difficult Yuki and Emma's feud was, hoping they would work through their issues on their own and not wanting to add my own troubles to the mix, but the fighting between my friends tormented my waking thoughts and crept into my dreams.

I woke night after night, skin beaded with sweat and sheets twisted into knots, from fevered nightmares. In one, Simon stood over Yuki's limp body, muzzle dripping blood from the bite wound in her neck. Even though it was only a dream, that image haunted me.

Things hadn't been the same between me and Simon since that dream. He assumed the tension between us was due to my disapproval of his relationship with Emma. I didn't disavow him of the notion. It was easier than trying to explain the true source of my unease.

And I was uncomfortable with his relationship with Emma, at least at first. Their behavior toward each other had gone from volatile to romantic, seemingly overnight. I assumed that it was a passing fling, one of many for Simon. But instead of Simon moving on, and Emma getting hurt, my pack lieutenant fell in love.

As far as I knew, Simon hadn't been in a serious relationship since Meredith. That didn't end well, not at all, but in that case it wasn't Simon's fault. Too bad no one at the time had been able to convince Simon of that.

Meredith had died and Simon was sucked into a tailspin of dangerous behavior. Drugs, crime—if it risked death, Simon had dabbled in it. He left university and hit the streets running. You could say that he never stopped running away from that fateful day, and the pain it caused him, until he came to Wakefield to help me and Yuki with our training.

Until he met Emma, and fell in love again.

I hadn't wanted to alienate Simon. I made him my pack lieutenant because I trusted him with my life. And though he could often be aggravating, I had come to value his friendship. I felt loyal to Simon and to my many years of friendship with Emma, but there was one person who came first.

Yuki would always come first in my life.

No matter what happens after graduation, Yuki would always be my soul mate. Even if Simon was correct, and I was no longer good for her, I'd leave her, but I'd never forget her. I would never stop loving Yuki.

She was everything to me.

But now that my pack, the small pack sharing the cabin with me, was beginning to come back together, I was less worried about the future.

I felt like I could breathe again.

Chapter 41
Yuki

I watched morning sunlight flicker across the brick walls of Wakefield High while Cal pulled his truck into a parking space. The school building seemed less like a house of horrors now and more like a small hill to climb—a minor speed bump to overcome. Well, a speed bump made of bad memories, overdue textbook reading assignments and missed homework.

Okay, maybe more like Mt. Everest, but I was hopeful. With Cal's steady presence, Emma's friendship, and Simon's grudging respect, I felt ready to face anything—even high school.

It's funny what a difference one day can make.

"You are so beautiful when you smile," Cal said, brushing the side of my cheek.

I hadn't realized that I was smiling, but now that he'd brought attention to it, I could feel a grin spread wide across my face. I had a hunch that I'd be doing a lot more smiling soon. High school was nearly over, and though I was still worried about the future, I'd started to form a plan for what I'd like to do when the summer ended.

Normally, when I looked at my calendar I noticed the moon phases first and the number of days until Samhain second. I hadn't given the future much thought beyond survival.

But that was no way to live.

Last night while fending off inevitable sleep, and the nightmares that it brings, I let my mind wander to happier thoughts. If I could do anything I wanted after high school, what would it be? That was a tough question. First, I made a mental list of my favorite things—Cal, my friends, art, anime, flea markets — then I fantasized about how these things could become my future.

Gordy was enrolled in a program for art and digital animation. He was following our love of anime and manga, and was really good at it too. But as much as I'd love to team up with Gordy on a manga project someday, I had a different focus.

Ever since my brush with death, I'd been able to see a glowing aura around ghosts. What if I used my artistic talent to paint unique pictures of something that no one else could see?

I loved the idea of painting something totally unique so much I bounced on the bed and had to cover my mouth with both hands to hold in a squee of excitement. I crept to my desk and sat up most of the night sketching out ideas.

There were a few places in Wakefield where I knew I could locate ghosts. Perhaps, I could find my muse while helping spirits of the dead find eternal peace. That idea made me ecstatically happy.

My daydreaming also involved getting a stall at my favorite flea market, for showing and selling my paintings. I could decorate the stall with black satin, no burgundy damask, no purple velvet—the possibilities seemed endless. In each scenario one thing remained constant; Cal was always by my side.

I leaned into Cal's hand, enjoying the rough feeling of his warm palm against my cool skin. Cal always ran hot. I was pretty sure it was a werewolf thing. I'd ask Emma if Simon was the same, but, you know, ewww. I was okay with them dating, sort of, but not quite ready for the intimate details.

"I had an epiphany last night," I said.

I turned my head to gaze into Cal's deep ocean eyes, his hand still cupping my cheek.

"About?" he asked, a lazy grin on his full lips.

Cal's voice had gone husky and I was having trouble concentrating, but it was important that I share my idea with him. I had been keeping too many secrets lately. It was time to start letting people back in, and I was starting with Cal.

"What do think about running an art stall in the flea market?" I asked.

"Will we be selling your art?" he asked, cocking an eyebrow. "I can finger paint at best."

I laughed remembering Cal's attempt at making a valentine card for me last February. In the attempted drawing, I looked like

Sasquatch, and a wolf that looked suspiciously like a poodle was holding an amorphous blob that was supposed to be his heart.

"My art, definitely," I said. "I have an entire concept, but as for decorating the stall, I'm torn between all black fabric or…"

Cal closed the distance between us, pressing his heated lips against my own. His hand brushed along my cheek as he slid his fingers into my hair. Time stopped. We were the only two people in the universe.

I leaned into Cal, enjoying our moment of bliss. I felt energized and relaxed, all at the same time. Cal was better than hot chocolate.

When he pulled away, my lips tingled. He kissed the bridge of my nose and leaned his forehead against mine.

"I love that idea," he said.

"So, if I create the paintings, you'll help me with the stall?" I asked breathlessly.

"Yes, I'll do anything you need," he said.

"Anything?" I asked.

"Anything," he said.

"Then kiss me," I said.

Chapter 42
Emma

I intercepted Yuki before her torturous daily trip past the supply closet. We hadn't had time to talk about her abduction, and the resulting panic attacks, but I wasn't letting my friend suffer this alone. Not anymore.

"Yo, Yuki, hold up," I shouted.

Yuki turned to face me, already appearing nervous about the prospect of running the supply closet gauntlet. Her pale face looked gray beneath a layer of rice powder, and a sheen of sweat beaded along her hairline. Her hands twisted the straps of her backpack in a vice-like grip. The black polish on her nails was scratched down to mere specks—never a good sign.

"Hey," she said. "What are you doing up here? Don't you have class downstairs?"

"Confession time," I said. "I finished my assignments...and have been working from the media room this period."

"H-how long have you been doing that?" she asked.

"Over a week," I said. I looked pointedly at the closet door visible past Yuki's shoulder. "I know about the panic attacks."

"Oh," she said.

Yuki looked away then lifted her chin to meet my gaze. There was something different about her today. She may still be anxious about walking past the door where her captors held her a few months ago, but I could see some of the old Yuki spunk in her eyes.

"Can I walk with you today?" I asked.

"I don't have to drink any of your teas, do I?" she asked, scrunching her nose.

"No," I said, chuckling. "No teas. Not today anyway."

"Cool," she said.

I stepped closer, ready to walk with her up the hall. I figured the best approach for today would be to keep Yuki distracted as we walked past the offending door.

"Are we on for library research this afternoon?" I asked.

I knew we talked about all of this last night, but I needed to get Yuki talking…and moving. Her breath came in rapid puffs, like a startled bird, but Yuki put one booted foot forward.

"Yeah," she said. "After school."

"Good," I said. "We need to try to save that girl, Sarah Randall. If we can discover the Grabber's identity, there's a possibility the authorities can get to him before he hurts her."

Yuki let go of the straps of her bag and clenched both hands into fists at her side. Her feet clomped against linoleum as she stomped across the floor.

"He's not going to touch that girl," she said. "Not if I can help it."

Yuki reached up to press one palm against her temple. She winced, but not at the memories that hid behind the supply room door. She didn't even look in that direction. No, I knew the signs of a headache. Yuki was suffering from another migraine, probably triggered by a powerful smell impression. Rose Hathaway must be agitated by our discussion.

If I'd been murdered and buried in the park, I'd be agitated too.

"Maybe Simon will have something for us by the time we reach the library," I said hopefully.

Simon had connections everywhere, some from his shady past and others from his skill at flirting with the opposite sex. I may be the library research queen, but Simon ruled the art of word of mouth. He was also king of the supernatural grapevine. If a photographer in the area had a reputation for violent or depraved behavior, Simon would find out.

"Cal said they may be late to the library," she said. "He wants to check out something my spirit guide said."

"And that was?" I asked.

"That the answers were in the ground," she said, shrugging. "My guide always talks in riddles, and I did find the skull in the ground, so I'm sure it's nothing. But Cal and Simon want to check the grave site for clues."

"They're not..." I said. I had to swallow a lump in my throat before continuing on. "They don't plan on digging her up, do they?"

"No," she said, shaking her head. "No way. I already asked and Cal said he wouldn't disturb the slumber of the dead. But he wants to search the ground around the skull, just in case I missed something. It was dark, and I was totally freaked out, so it's possible that there are still clues out there waiting to be found."

I pictured Calvin and Simon scratching at the earth around the shallow grave and shuddered.

"I'd much rather stick to library research," I said.

"I couldn't agree with you more," she said. "I'd rather wrestle with flying monkeys than go back there while the Grabber remains free." She touched her head again and winced. "Not really a big fan of smell attacks either. This headache is killing me. I'll leave sniffing around creeptastic grave sites to Cal."

The door to Yuki's class came into view and I smiled.

"Well, I'll see you after school," I said.

Yuki's brow furrowed and her lips paled.

"Aren't you going to walk me to class?" she asked.

"Already did," I said. I pointed at the classroom door. "See you after final period."

"Son of a dung beetle," she muttered. "How did she do that?"

It was the last thing I heard Yuki say as she shuffled into her class, a dazed smile on her face.

Chapter 43
Calvin

I grinned as I reread the text from Yuki. *Emma giving me ride 2 library. C U there!*

I was happy that Emma and Yuki were hanging out again. It was also a relief to know that Yuki was safely away from the grave site. My pack scouts hadn't seen anyone approach the area, but the Grabber could show up at any time.

Part of me wanted him to show up.

I let out a low growl and stalked into the clearing. My wolf pushed its way to the surface, struggling to break free. I closed my eyes and took a steadying breath, letting my wolf senses heighten without fully shifting. The full moon was drawing close, weakening my control.

I was new to my werewolf abilities, a mere pup as Simon continually reminded me, but I was also pack alpha. With pack members nearby, I had to demonstrate my dominance. Involuntarily losing control of my wolf would be seen as a sign of weakness.

And if I changed fully into my wolf form this close to the full moon, I may not be able to change back. Missing finals week was unacceptable, and I didn't think my teachers would let a wolf sit for my exams.

So I focused on the changes within my body and fought to exert my will over my wolf half. *Soon*, I promised. I would travel north to the hundreds of acres of Maine woods the pack owned, as soon as the Grabber was found and graduation was over. There I could run and hunt without fear of humans.

But I wasn't on pack land. I was in a public park and would not risk the secret of my people because of a lack of control.

Eyes closed, I visualized the changes within myself. I began at my feet and worked my way up through my body, and the corresponding chakras. My body relaxed as I visualized sending all tension and negative thoughts out through the crown of my head as white light, to return to the earth mother to be cleansed. My wolf was hovering at the surface, but we were now at peace with each other.

I opened my eyes to a vivid riot of color. The clearing itself had not changed, but I had. I remained in human form, but now my senses were heightened by the close presence of my wolf spirit.

The vibrant red of the roses seemed painfully bright as they wound their way up the moss covered stone wall. It was no wonder that Yuki chose this location to paint. A breeze carried the scent of roses to my wolf-enhanced nose, and birds sang in the trees. The place would have been a tranquil place for a picnic, if not for the skull peeking out of the soil.

I scanned the ground looking for clues as Simon loped into the clearing. The snorting sounds from his direction, as he scented the air, seemed unnaturally loud to my sensitive ears. Simon was our most skilled tracker. If the killer had been here recently, he would be able to catch his scent.

"Anything?" I asked. I didn't take my eyes from the ground, continuing to search for anything the killer may have left behind.

"Sorry, mate," he said. "There's nothing here. Just Yuki's scent all over the clearing and park trail. I can smell the paints she used, some snack food she must have brought here, and the chain oil from her bicycle, but nothing helpful. The crime is too old and the Grabber hasn't returned here recently."

A pebble shot toward me as Simon kicked the gravel path with his expensive shoes. His frustration was beginning to show, if you knew where to look. He may try to act indifferent, but Simon had a sympathetic streak for hard cases. His time living on the streets had taught him the horrors that humans can inflict upon each other, especially on the weak. Simon wanted to rescue Sarah Randall from the Grabber, but we had to find him first.

"Don't worry, man," I said. "We will find the Grabber, and we'll save that girl."

I crouched, examining the ground at the base of the rock wall. I could see pieces of candy and trail mix scattered near the skull and imagined the hand that held the snack food flailing as Yuki realized the pale object in front of her wasn't rock, but human bone.

In the shadow of the wall, something caught my eye. Running my hands along the mossy ground, I found a small piece of paper sticking out of the rock wall. The paper was thick, the type used for high quality business cards or party invitations. Only one corner remained. The only reason it survived the passage of time at all was its location wedged between the stones, where a rough protrusion created a natural shelf from the elements.

"Do you have a pair of tweezers with you?" I asked.

"Of course," Simon said.

With a flourish, Simon withdrew a grooming kit from his coat pocket. He was wearing his leather jacket, even though temperatures had climbed into the eighties today. I don't know how he can stand it. Werewolves run hot. I was suffering in a cotton t-shirt and paper thin pair of jeans.

Using tweezers, I grabbed hold of the piece of paper and slowly wiggled it from side to side. With a soft sound, like the whisper of dry leaves caught in a breeze, the paper came free. Moving out of the wall's shadow, I held it up to the light. The only thing remaining on the card was a sunburst insignia.

"There's no text," I said, shaking my head. "But maybe we can trace this symbol."

"It's more than we had," Simon said. He tilted his head to the sky and let out a heavy sigh. "Okay, let's go see what the girls have found. Maybe this will make more sense once we have information on photographers who have worked in Wakefield."

I remembered the words of Mahatma Ghandi and felt a stirring of hope. *When I despair, I remember that all through history the ways of truth and love have always won. There have been tyrants, and murderers, and for a time they can seem invincible, but in the end they always fall.*

Leaving Rose Peterson in this shallow grave might have been the beginning of the Grabber's downfall. With the smell impressions that Yuki sensed and the sunburst symbol to go on, we have a chance of catching this murderer.

I smiled at the card in my hand. *In the end they always fall.*

Chapter 44
Yuki

I rubbed my neck and groaned.

"I feel like my eyes are bleeding," I said. "I so totally need a break."

Emma and I had been scouring yearbooks, newspapers, and phone books looking for the names of photographers who had photographed Wakefield events in the past. We were focusing on school events like graduation, but the number of names increased by the minute.

The list was huge.

I wished we could call Gordy and Katie for research help, but Katie's parents were freaking out over reports of the Graduation Grabber being back in town. When Gordy's uncle offered for them to stay with his family for the weekend, Katie's parents jumped at the chance. They picked up Gordy and Katie from school and drove straight to the beach house.

I thought it might be kind of awkward for Katie, hanging out with both Gordy's family and her parents, but she sounded excited when they told us about it over lunch. Apparently, she was planning on putting both families to work, preparing for the graduation party there the following weekend.

We could have used their help with our search for the Grabber, but I guess it was for the best. It was hard to keep the secret of my psychic gift, and the fact I'm dating a werewolf, from Gordy and Katie. But there were so many sources to check, and I felt like we were running out of time.

I groaned again.

Warm hands rested on my shoulders and began kneading away the knots of tension. Cal. He leaned in and kissed the skin behind my ear, sending a shiver up my spine.

"Miss me?" he asked.

"Always," I said, turning to look into his smiling face. He was wearing a familiar toothy grin, but beneath the surface he looked tired. Maybe we all needed a break.

I turned to Emma to plead my case, but she was lip locked with Simon. *So gross.* I needed brain bleach, stat.

Focusing on Cal was so much better, and much less likely to make me vomit on the book in front of me.

"Find anything spooktacular at the park?" I asked.

I avoided saying "at Rose's grave," but the ghost perked up anyway, producing a burst of smell and sending a shooting pain to join its friends behind my eyes.

"Just this," he said.

Cal set a plastic sandwich bag on the desk. Inside the clear bag was a small piece of dark paper. I reached out with shaking hands and lifted the bag to the light, turning it to look at both sides of the heavy paper. It looked like the corner of a business card.

Emma, finished with her kissing, leaned in for a closer look.

"What is it?" she asked.

"A clue, love," Simon said, waggling his eyebrows.

Emma punched him playfully on the hip and turned to Cal. He was more likely to give us straight answers.

"It looks like some kind of symbol, maybe from a business logo or personal insignia," he said.

Emma slid her chair closer and I licked my lips and fidgeted in my seat. If we could match up that symbol with one of the photographer's ads, we'd know who the Grabber was.

We'd be able to save Sarah Randall.

Moth wings fluttered in my belly as I daydreamed about rescuing the Grabber's current victim. No one should have to suffer the nightmare of being kidnapped, but at least if we solved the mystery of the Grabber's identity, we could save her life. It would take time to get over the trauma, but she'd survive.

I should know.

All thoughts of taking a break were gone. My earlier fatigue was forgotten as we flipped back through phone book yellow pages, hoping to find a match for the mysterious symbol.

Unfortunately, this was a dead end.

"That was the last one," Emma said, pushing the thick phone book aside.

She pinched the bridge of her nose and yawned.

"Time for a drive?" I asked. I held up our list of names and business addresses. "We could visit each of these locations. Maybe we'll get lucky and the symbol will be posted on a sign or shop window."

My stomach growled like an angry wendigo. I pressed a hand to my middle, wishing I'd brought more trail mix. I'd already eaten the emergency rations I kept in my backpack. I should have known better than to bring just one bag. Research made me hungry.

Simon snorted and Emma laughed.

"I think it's time for dinner," Cal said.

He smiled down at me, blue eyes shining through shaggy hair. I was hungry, but I wasn't going to give up on finding Sarah Randall. We didn't have time for a sit down meal, but there were other options.

"Okay, let's grab take-out," I said. "If we use the drive-thru at Mr. Green Genes, we can search for the symbol while we eat."

"Are we all going in my car?" Emma asked.

We'd never all fit in Cal's truck, and there's no way I'd ride on Simon's motorcycle, so the question was valid. If we decided to ride together, Emma's car was our only choice. But should we split up and cover more ground? I felt safer with us all working together, but if it meant that Sarah Randall had a better chance of survival if we split up, then that's what we would do.

"We'll cover more ground if we go in pairs," I said. I handed half the list to Emma. "You take Simon and I'll go with Cal. Call if you find anything."

As an added bonus, I wouldn't have to witness Simon eat. The plan was made of win.

Chapter 45
Simon

There were too many addresses to check in one night. The list that Emma held had more names than my little black book.

That is really saying something.

Emma and Yuki had included photographers whose business locations were outside of Wakefield and yet had worked here for a few seasonal events. This was based on the theory that the Graduation Grabber was not a resident of Wakefield, but had a reason to come here during the month of June when he used it as his hunting grounds.

As far as theories go, it wasn't half bad. Even my wolf spirit knows instinctually that you don't foul your own den.

But the addresses outside of Wakefield were too far afield to canvas in one night. So we had begun with the businesses within the local zip code. Unfortunately, the starburst symbol was nowhere to be found.

At midnight, after hours of searching, we decided to call it a night. Strands of Emma's silky hair had escaped the twist at the back of her neck and the paper that the list was written on was now wrung into a small wad of accordion folds. The excitement of the chase had fizzled into an exhausting, monotonous tension.

While driving Emma home, I knew that she was not in the mood to discuss our future, but recent events had triggered my protective instincts and I let myself succumb to my emotions.

"Stay with me," I said.

My hands tightened on the wheel as a lump formed in my throat.

"What?" Emma asked.

"After graduation," I said. "Don't leave. I don't think I can bear your absence. I need you with me, where I can protect you. So, stay with me."

"Oh Simon," she said. Emma reached out and touched my face, brushing along the scar on my cheek until her hand rested on my arm. "I love you too."

I sucked in a breath. I knew that Emma cared about me, but until this moment I hadn't heard those words from her lips. My heart filled, then fluttered. I did love Emma, but my feelings often terrified me.

The pain of loss is unbearable when you truly love someone.

"Will you stay with me?" I asked.

I held my breath and waited. The silence seemed to drag on while streetlamps marked the passage of time as one by one they ghosted overhead.

"No," she said.

"But…" I said.

"Wait, let me explain," she said. Emma grimaced. "It's not you, it's me."

Was she breaking up with me? If so, I was a bloody fool to fall in love again. It always ended badly.

"You haven't done anything wrong," she said, clenching her hands into fists. Emma lifted her chin and sat up straight, meeting my glance. "And I understand why you want me to stay. I would have asked you to come with me, but I realize the importance of your duties to the pack."

"You want me to go with you?" I asked.

"Yes, but I know that you can't," she said.

It was true. As much as it pained me, I couldn't leave Cal and the pack behind. I had sworn an oath and I wouldn't go back on my word. I would miss Emma while she was away at school, but at least now I knew that she'd be missing me too.

"You're right, love," I said. I let out a heavy sigh. "I can't stray far from the pack. They need me."

"And I need to go," she said. Emma's lower lip trembled, but she squared her shoulders and stared straight ahead. "I've dreamed about becoming a veterinarian, being able to help sick and injured animals. This is what I've wanted for a long time. And now with the pack, I have a job waiting for me when I graduate college. I won't let this chance pass me by."

I realized then that I'd been wrong to ask Emma to stay. She was strong and could take care of herself. We would survive the long distance relationship, and when she graduated we would both be working toward the same goal. Together we could ensure the safety of the pack.

How did I end up with such a perfect mate?

"God, I love you," I said. There, I'd done it. The words were out and I was committed. But if I was honest with myself, I'd been committed to this relationship since the moment I met Emma. When it came to my feelings, I was a slow learner. "And, I support you."

"Like I said before," she said. Emma's shoulders relaxed and she leaned in close, lips parting. "I love you too."

Chapter 46
Yuki

I lay tangled in my sheets, clutching a dung beetle plushie to my chest. I needed a good night's sleep if we were going to continue our search for the Graduation Grabber and the missing girl Sarah Randall, but I felt too wired. Staring at the ceiling, I counted the glow-in-the-dark stars that Cal had put above my bed ages ago. He'd placed them in constellations; the Big Dipper, Centaurus, Hercules, Draco, Aquarius, Ursa Major, Hydra…

Huh, sleep came after all.

Too bad it was a nightmare. I opened my eyes to see a stack of cardboard boxes swim across my vision. The room was all too familiar.

I was in the school supply closet, and I wasn't alone.

Someone held my wrists behind my back with large, sweaty hands while his teammates taunted me. The room was small and each wall was lined with oversized football players. Their nylon jerseys swished as they puffed out their chests and flexed their muscles. *Neanderthals.*

This time, I kept my comments to myself. I'd learned that my dream tormenters were even more cruel than their real-life counterparts. I bit my lip and waited for what would come next. But instead of the usual threats from the J-team, and Zempter's lengthy evil-villain monologue, a girl floated toward me.

She was young, pale…and covered in blood.

"Roses are red," she said, laughing. I was pretty sure that this was Rose Peterson, and the blood covering her was definitely red. Subtle she was not. "Violets are blue. I died at the hands of the Grabber…and YOU WILL TOO."

She disappeared in a burst of golden sparkles, leaving the cloying scent of roses. Where she had stood, or creepily floated, sat a girl I hadn't met, but recognized as Sarah Randall. Her wrists and ankles were bound with rope and tears ran down her face to soak the filthy cloth tied in her mouth.

"Don't cry," I said. I knew my tormenters would punish me for speaking, but I had to try to comfort her. "I'll save you."

The jocks started laughing and the room spun. Harsh fluorescent light shone on shark teeth that flashed from cruel mouths.

"Freak," Jared Zempter said. He spat on the floor at my feet. "How can you save her, if you can't even save yourself?"

"Yes, dear," a witch said, appearing from behind one of the boxes. She was one of three witches from another familiar nightmare. Great, now my nemeses were joining forces in my sleep. "You cannot save them. Not unless you return the amulet."

Ever since "borrowing" Nera's amulet, an amulet with magical powers to protect the wearer from spirits of the dead, from an occult shop rumored to be owned by witches, I'd had nightmares about the witches coming for what was theirs. In every dream, my friends died and I became engulfed in rivers of their blood.

Yeah, not fun.

Gnarled, talon-tipped fingers clawed at my chest, searching for the amulet. I struggled to pull away, but the jock behind me held tight to my wrists. Jared Zempter pulled a long, wicked blade from his belt and came to tower over me.

"We are going to have so much fun with this one," he said, a cruel smile twisting his lips.

Jared never went anywhere without backup, but his friend wasn't Jay Freeman, the other half of the J-team. The man standing with him looked older, but his face was a blank canvas. He lifted his own knife and a whimper escaped from Sarah Randall's hunched form.

I knew who Jared's new friend was. The man looming over me was the Graduation Grabber.

With a shriek, I kicked out at my assailants…and tumbled out of the supply closet into another realm. A warm breeze tickled my face and whispered through the dry grass where I now sat. I was in limbo, the dream-like space between our world and the ever-after.

But how did I end up here?

"What are you doing here, child?" my spirit guide asked. A gigantic dung beetle towered above me, antennae twitching. "I was not expecting you."

"Um, I don't know," I said, brushing dirt off my pajamas.

In the supply closet, I'd been in my usual Goth attire, but now I was in the pink skull pj's I'd gone to sleep in. I looked down to see Jack Skellington slippers on my feet. Right, I definitely was wearing boots when I kicked out at Jared Zempter, the witch, and the Grabber. Could this night get any weirder?

"I smell fear on you, little one," my spirit guide said. Its arms waved in the air above my head. "Do not allow fear to blind you. Open your eyes and follow the words of the snake, the cry of the cat, and the rays of the sun."

I opened my eyes, blinking up at the constellations above my bed. Follow the words of the snake, the cry of the cat, and the rays of the sun. Oh yeah, like that wasn't vague or anything.

Why do spirit guides have to be so fond of riddles?

After my sucktastic night of spooky nightmares and cryptic dreams, I was exhausted. Too bad the sun was creeping its way across my bed. It was time to get up and start the day.

It was time to find the Grabber.

Chapter 47
Emma

I yawned as I plunked myself down beside the snake cage. After a night out searching for the Grabber, I was worn out. I rubbed at my sore neck and grabbed the morning reports, scanning for anything important.

The animal shelter where I volunteer is a small facility, but it provides services for all of Yorkshire County. Funding had dried up, which meant we were understaffed and overworked. Other local shelters had closed their doors, so we were all that was left.

Saturday mornings were chaos, which is why I chose that day to volunteer. It was when the shelter needed me most. But today I was weary of the kennel. During weekend shifts, the sound of dogs barking never waned as potential owners scouted for the perfect pet to adopt. Not many people came into the reptile room, which is why I sought refuge here.

Well, one of the reasons.

The reptile room was a quiet respite from the echoing walls of the kennels, and busy adoption frenzy at the front desk, but that wasn't the only reason I came here when I was stressed. The snakes calmed me.

When snakes first started talking to me, I had avoided them. But recently I discovered that their presence was soothing. Duvet, the boa constrictor who sat in the cage at my elbow, often whispered to me. Its sibilant voice was calming.

Yeah, I know, I'm the crazy snake lady.

I flipped through the reports, checking the lists for recent adoptions, new arrivals, and calls for animal control. Since there was no funding our county didn't have an animal control officer, so calls often came to the shelter or went to the police. Ultimately, we learned of any strays, but dealing with them was another story. "Collection duty" was left to volunteers willing to take the risk.

Scanning the logs, I found multiple reports of an animal noise complaint. Repeated complaints had been called in three nights ago. Residents of an apartment complex in the neighboring town of Sansborough had reported loud wailing and crying from a stray cat that woke them from their sleep. The address of the apartment building was at 115 Sheridan Street.

That address niggled. I reread the report—115 Sheridan Street, Sansborough Maine—and seeing the full street address pushed a memory to the surface. Wasn't there a photography studio on Sheridan Street?

Holding the report in a white knuckled grip, I strode to the nearby break room. I pulled my messenger bag from the cabinet below the coffee maker and quickly retrieved our list from last night's search.

Goosebumps rose along my arms. One of the photography studios on the list was located at 117 Sheridan Street. *Oh em geesss.*

That was no stray cat. The crying that pulled residents from their beds three nights ago wasn't from a feline—that voice was human.

We had found Sarah Randall.

Chapter 48
Calvin

Yuki bounced in her seat, fork splashing strawberry juice from her waffles onto the table, as she spoke rapidly on the phone. Usually I gave Yuki her privacy and tuned out my werewolf hearing, but it was obvious that Emma had some exciting information.

Had she found a clue to the Grabber's identity?

Leave it to Emma to manage research while working. During her shift at the animal shelter, Emma had read reports of a stray cat in Sansborough, outside an apartment building at 115 Sheridan Street—beside one of the photography studios on our list. No one had reported seeing an actual cat. The residents who called it in, complained of a cat waking them from their sleep as it wailed outside their building. The event took place three nights ago, the same day Sarah Randall went missing.

Emma had pieced the clues together and called another volunteer to finish out her shift at the shelter. That was when she had called Yuki, making her splash sticky syrup all over the glass covered tablecloth.

I had taken Yuki out for breakfast hoping that waffles covered in ice cream and strawberry syrup would coax her to eat. Being actively plagued by a ghost, even one whose smell impression wasn't a foul stench, often made it difficult for Yuki to eat.

Plus, I suspected that Emma's concerns over Yuki's mental health were accurate. When I picked her up this morning she looked as though she spent the entire night wrestling with her demons. She may wear dramatic makeup, but the dark circles around Yuki's eyes weren't completely intentional.

But Yuki was awake now and smiling from ear to ear. I matched her smile with my own and flagged down our waitress to

pay our check. Emma was on her way and Simon would join us
before we left town.

It was time to rescue Sarah Randall.

"You were listening, right?" Yuki said.

Yuki ended the call with Emma and continued to bounce in
her seat. She clapped her hands and smiled, looking like a little
kid—a kid wearing a spiked collar and red lipstick. It was
unbelievable cute.

"Yes," I said. "Sounds like Emma discovered a potential
location for the Grabber. That was some quick reasoning."

"I know, like, she's totally amazing," she said.

Yuki happily scooped up a forkful of ice cream smothered
waffle and put it in her mouth with a contented sigh.

"She's not the only one," I said. I leaned across the table
and kissed Yuki, licking away the whipped cream at the corner of
her mouth. "And you're twice as sweet."

Yuki swallowed and a hint of pink showed through her
white face powder.

"Only you would call me sweet, Calvin Miller," she said.

I took in her appearance, dressed all in black with spikes at
her neck and wrists. No, not everyone would think Yuki was
sweet, but that's just because they don't bother to look beneath the
surface. And they don't kiss her while she's eating waffles.

"I promise to do so every Saturday henceforth, my Dung
Beetle Princess," I said, standing and bowing at the waist.

Yuki groaned.

"Oh no, don't start that again," she said.

I took her hand and pulled her to her feet. She gasped as I
stole another kiss. Someone at a booth behind ours started
clapping.

"…mmm," she said. That's embarrassing"

"Embarrassing?" I asked, cocking an eyebrow.

"Yeah, embarrassing, but yummy," she said. "People are
staring. Let's get out of here."

"After you, Princess," I said. With a flourish, I gestured to
the door. "Your carriage awaits."

Chapter 49
Yuki

Emma pulled her car to the curb and I tried to ignore Simon's arm across her shoulders. We had decided to car pool, leaving Cal's truck and Simon's motorcycle back at the Wakefield Park and Ride. As we came to a stop, my stomach fluttered. Hopefully one more car on the busy street would go unnoticed.

Turning away from Emma and Simon, I looked out the side window. We were parallel parked directly across the street from the apartment complex where residents had called in reports of a wailing cat. Sansborough was a former mill town and we were in an old downtown section where Victorian homes with gingerbread trim sat like fancy debutantes beside stark brick buildings, shabby gas stations, and vacant warehouses.

The apartment complex was a five story modern structure with cheery yellow clapboard siding and small weathered balconies covered in lawn chairs and potted plants. A chain link fence encircled a small lot to the right of the building where large signs proclaimed parking for tenants only. An alley ran alongside the apartments to the left.

Squatting in the shadows of the alley was a van, its back doors facing the road. And painted across those doors was a familiar sunburst symbol.

I rubbed my eyes and looked again. Nope, not a hallucination brought on from wishful thinking. We had found the sunburst symbol from the card left at the burial site—a logo for Bright Star Photography.

"You all see that, right?" I asked.

Emma sucked in a breath and Cal squeezed my hand.

"That sign is displaying a suspiciously familiar looking symbol," Simon said.

Sign? I looked away from the alley to examine the
building beside the van. From a wrap-around porch hung a
wooden sign announcing Bright Star Photography on the same
sunburst background as the van.

"We are definitely at the right place," Emma said.

The photography studio sat behind a white picket fence.
The studio had once been a home, but the house, like many
buildings on this street, had been converted into a business. I
wondered if the Grabber lived in the rooms above. I looked for
signs of life in the dormer windows, but nothing moved behind the
white lace curtains.

"This place is creepy," I said. "Knowing the Grabber
works here…it's like Leave It To Beaver meets the Mansons."

"You'd prefer the Addams Family?" Simon asked.

"Hells yes," I said. "This place looks like someone's
grandmother's house. The kind who bakes cookies and hands out
candy apples at Halloween—the ones *without* razor blades."

"Looks can be deceiving," Cal said.

"You got that right," Emma said. She shook her head then
froze. Her lips parted and she leaned forward. "Yuki, didn't you
say your ghost smelled like lanolin?"

"Yeah, the rose smell is strongest and the chemical smell
burns my nose, but there's a hint of lanolin," I said. "You know,
like that sweater my mom made when she was going through her
knitting phase."

"I told you not to wear it in the rain," Emma said with a
snort. "Well, I think I know why your ghost smells like that."

"You do?" I asked.

"Yes," she said, pointing. "The store on the corner of that
brick building, just past the picket fence, is a yarn shop. Their sign
says they specialize in all natural, handspun yarns."

"Like the yarn my mom used to make that sweater," I said.

"The kind that smells like sheep," Emma said.

*****

Locating the Grabber's lair was exciting. Waiting around
looking for an excuse to call the cops was not. For the gazillionth
time, I sighed.

"Why can't we just go in there and storm the castle?" I asked, waving my hand toward the studio.

"This isn't one of your role playing games," Simon said. Was that a sneer? Gah, that guy made me crazy. "We can't just blaze into someone's home or business, in broad daylight, on Main Street."

"Senility kicking in already?" I asked. "We're not on Main Street, old man. This is Sheridan Street."

"Semantics," he said. "And I am not old. I'm mature, like a fine wine."

"Oh my God you two," Emma said. She squeezed her eyes shut and clenched her fists. "Shut. Up."

"Maybe Yuki and I should take a walk around the block," Cal said. "We can pick up snacks somewhere, and get a chance to look at things from a different vantage point."

And the walk would get me out of kicking distance from Simon. Good thinking. I was ready to stomp all over his fancy clothes with my dirty boots, while he was still wearing them. Seriously, if there was a Hell, it would be me trapped for eternity in a small space with Simon.

"Go," Emma said. "We'll keep watch."

I jumped out of the car faster than you can say "flying monkeys" and skipped over to where Cal waited on the sidewalk. He reached for my hand and I let out a huge breath as we started walking away from Emma's car.

"Better?" Cal asked. His thumb brushed circles along the sensitive skin on my wrist.

"Much better," I said, briefly bowing my head. "How do you live with him?"

"Simon?" he asked. "He's not so bad, once you get past the cocky posturing and his tendency to hog the bathroom mirror."

"Too bad we couldn't turn him into a vampire," I said. "Creatures of the night can't see their reflection. Simon would totally freak."

Cal snorted.

We continued to walk along Sheridan Street, discreetly stealing glances at Bright Star Photography. It killed me that we couldn't just barge in there looking for signs of Sarah Randall. My chest felt tight as I imagined her tied up in one of those rooms.

"So what are we waiting for exactly?" I asked.

"For the guy to do something suspicious that we can report to the police," he said. "He doesn't know we're watching him, so hopefully he'll make a mistake."

"What if he does something and there's no time for the police," I asked.

"Then Simon and I go in and help the girl," he said. Cal stopped, feet firmly planted, and tipped my chin up so that my eyes met his. "But if that happens, I want you to promise me that you and Emma will stay in the car."

"But why?" I asked. "We can help."

"Because this guy is dangerous," he said. "Neither of you have werewolf healing. Plus, Simon and I won't be able to concentrate on saving Sarah Randall if we're worrying about you."

"Oh," I said. "Okay, fine, but if you rescue her, we're helping once she's in the car."

"You do know there's a chance it's too late," Cal said, squeezing my hand.

Tears welled up, making me feel foolish.

"Of course I do," I said.

But really, I hadn't let myself think about it. We would find Sarah Randall alive. We just had to.

Chapter 50
Simon

Emma woke with a choking gasp beside me. It was getting dark and we'd started taking naps and going for food in shifts. I had settled in for a long wait.

"It's alright, love," I said. "Nothing's happened."

Emma tilted her head back against the head-rest and sighed.

"Stakeouts are b-o-r-i-n-g," Yuki said from the back seat. "On TV this guy would have done something incriminating in, like, thirty seconds."

"That is because of the insufficient attention span of the average viewer," I said, looking pointedly at Yuki.

She crossed her arms and harrumphed, stomping her foot on the floorboards.

"Patience young Padawan," Cal said.

"I really do not understand you two," I said, shaking my head.

"Wait," Emma said. "Look."

A beam of light cut across the alley as someone at the photography studio opened a side door and poked their head outside.

"Is that the Grabber?" Yuki whispered.

No one else dared break the silence that hung thick in the car. I held my breath, muscles coiled and ready to strike. If anyone threatened Emma, they'd soon regret it.

Motion in the alley broke me from my protective thoughts. A tall man went to the driver's side of the van and, after looking up and down the alley, opened the door. Stepping onto the running boards he leaned in and started the engine. As soon as the engine roared, he jumped back down and hurried to the rear of the van.

The man looked sinister in the red glow of the tail lights. He looked to be of average weight, but was tall, approximately six foot five. Shadows played along the alley, giving the man a reed thin evil twin who danced maniacally across the walls.

I shifted my focus from the shadows, to the man himself. Even with my enhanced vision it was difficult to tell his age from this distance, but at a guess, I'd say he was in his fifties. He wore a dress shirt, but had pulled large hiking boots on over his khaki pants. Opening the rear doors of the van, he pulled out a rain parka which he slipped over his head.

Darting glances toward the road, he withdrew yellow rubber gloves from the pockets and pulled those on as well. He spread a sheet of plastic across the floor of the van and used a long-handled shovel to weigh it down. On the other side of the plastic, he set a backpack to keep the sheeting in place.

The backpack was covered in pink and yellow daisies.

"I know that not every man has my impeccable sense of fashion, but I don't think that backpack is his," I said, stifling a growl. "And those boots? I would swear he was a loafer man."

"All the more reason to think he's twisted," Yuki said. "Loafers are evil."

"Oh my God, you guys," Emma said. "I think he's getting rid of her."

"Yes, it's time we end this," Calvin said. "It's too late to call the police.

Calvin was right. We had waited all day for the man to do something and now that his behavior was overtly suspicious, it was too late to wait for backup. If we left this to the authorities, Sarah Randall would be dead.

In fact, she may be already.

I growled, allowing my wolf to surface. If anyone looked into my face now, they'd see the predatory gaze and terrifying fangs of a wolf. Good. I wanted this monster to know fear. I wanted him to feel the same kind of terror he inflicted on his victims.

"Stay in the car, love," I said. I brushed Emma's arm, not daring to squeeze her hand. I wanted to reassure her, not break her fingers.

"You too," Calvin said, turning to Yuki. "No matter what happens. If something goes wrong, call the cops and drive away from here."

"I'm not leaving Simon," Emma said. She had the steering wheel in a white-knuckled grip.

"He's right," I said. "Stay in the car. But don't worry, we won't be but a moment. You won't even have time to miss us."

With a signal from Calvin, I lunged from the car and raced toward the alley. In the brief moment while we had talked, the man had ducked back inside the building. He now carried a struggling form.

I held up my hand, motioning for Calvin to wait. It wouldn't do to have the man drop the girl. She was covered with a wool blanket, but I saw a flash of feet bound together. Her hands were probably bound as well. If she fell, she'd have no way to shield her fall.

We crouched in the shadows, waiting for our chance to strike.

The man closed the short distance from the building to the van and roughly shoved the girl onto the plastic sheeting. He raised one hand to close the rear doors of the van and paused to gloat over his handy work.

That pause would be his undoing.

Chapter 51
Yuki

There was something ridiculous about the man wearing bright rubber gloves like my mom uses while washing dishes. A laugh bubbled up and I clapped a hand over my mouth. *Get a grip.*

As Cal and Simon ghosted across the street, melting into the shadows, the Grabber stepped back inside the open photography studio door. A moment later, he returned carrying a large, blanket wrapped bundle. Something, or rather someone, struggled beneath the blanket.

I felt like someone had kicked me in the stomach, knocking all the wind out of my lungs and making bile rise in my throat. A pair of bound ankles swung out from the blanket and I let out a high pitched mew.

"It's alright, Yuki," Emma whispered. "Cal and Simon will save her."

But it wasn't alright. It felt like nothing would be right again. My lungs tightened further and beads of cold sweat rolled down my back.

The Grabber tossed the bundle into the back of the van, like discarded trash. But the bundle wasn't trash, it was Sarah Randall.

Sarah was tied at the wrists and ankles with rope that shone white against her dark jeans and long sleeved t-shirt. Thank the gods for small favors—she was fully clothed.

Emma's car felt like a coffin. I struggled for breath and my hands fisted. I needed to get out of the car. I had to save that girl.

I swore while bound in that supply closet that if given the chance, I'd never let that happen to anyone again. I wouldn't allow bullies to hurt another kid from my school. Graduation may be around the corner, but I had one more victim to save.

I burst from the car and into the street.

Light came from nowhere and I heard the squeal of tires on pavement. I'd run into the street uncaring for my own safety. I had been so focused on rescuing the girl from her bonds, that I'd dashed into the road without looking.

Lesson learned; always look both ways when crossing the street. I'd remember that, if I survived the night.

My body flew through the air to land hard on the pavement. The road felt warm against my face, still holding the heat of the day.

So many small details became vivid in that one moment. Sarah Randall was missing a shoe—the one bare foot shaking as she cried. Simon's fury as he slammed the Grabber against the ground. The cloying scent of roses as Rose Peterson's ghost witnessed her revenge and waited for me to guide her into the light. Would I be joining her? I really did feel awful.

Then everything else was eclipsed by the blue of Cal's eyes as he hovered over me.

"Cal," I said. A cough wracked my body.

"Don't try to talk," Cal said. "Emma's coming, and I called an ambulance."

"I'm…sorry," I said. I felt a traitorous tear escape and run down into my hair. I didn't want to cry. "I love you."

"I love you too," he said.

Cal squeezed my hand and Emma's blond hair came into view.

"If you live through this, I swear I'm going to kill you," she said.

Chapter 52
Emma

"Hold pressure there," I said.

I pointed to a cut along Yuki's hairline, instructing Calvin as I made a cursory search of her other injuries. Leave it to Yuki to run headlong into an oncoming vehicle. Luckily for her, it was only a moped.

Still, I didn't dare move her.

I removed an inflatable neck brace from its packaging and pulled the tab to inflate. Circling Yuki's neck with the brace, I looked into her eyes. They were pinched together in pain, but her pupils looked even and responsive as I moved my hand in front of them to shield them from the moped's headlight.

Someone behind me kept saying how sorry they were. Oh right, the driver. I'd have to take a look at his injuries too. But first I had to get Yuki stable and then see to Sarah Randall.

Simon was doing his best, but he had his hands full…literally.

I had watched as Simon turned toward the road and witnessed Yuki's foolish bolt from the car. It had all seemed to happen in slow motion. I tried to move, to leap from the car to Yuki's aid, but my muscles froze. Simon flinched as the moped collided with Yuki's path. He turned to Cal who was already racing into the street. With a nod to himself, he turned back to the Grabber.

Cal and I would help Yuki, the Grabber was his.

In a blur of werewolf speed, Simon tackled the Grabber to the ground. A grim smile tugged at his lips as he pressed the man's face into the filthy ground of the alley. Seeing that Simon was okay, and the Grabber apprehended, my muscles came alive. I fumbled with the door latch and sprinted into the street.

It all happened within seconds, but it felt like an eternity.

I knelt beside Yuki, hoping that her injuries were superficial. She seemed to be having trouble breathing, but it didn't sound like a punctured lung. If I had to make a guess, I'd say she was having an anxiety attack.

Guilt twisted my stomach. I had known that Yuki was having a hard time reliving her own abduction. I should have anticipated her reaction to finding Sarah Randall. Seeing the girl bound and gagged, with her tormentor leering, must have pushed Yuki over the edge. It was too similar to her recent experience. An experience she hadn't fully recovered from.

"Is...is she okay?" Yuki asked.

"Shhh," Calvin said.

"It's alright," I said. I forced a smile and packed up my bag. "I'm going to check on her now. Just don't move."

"Okay," she said.

"Keep her safe," I said to Calvin. "I'll be right back."

The guy on the moped paced back and forth in the road. He looked alright, but I probably should try to calm him down.

"Are you okay?" I asked.

"Me?" he asked. "Sure. I'm fine. My ride's fine too. But, did I, like, kill that girl? Is she okay? I was just going out to grab a pizza."

The guy looked like he was a few years older than me. He probably attended nearby Sansborough College.

"She'll be okay," I said. "I've called an ambulance, so don't go anywhere. The police are coming too and, after the paramedics check you over, they'll want a statement. Maybe you can direct traffic while we wait for them to get here?"

"Sure," he said, continuing his pacing.

College guy's comments had given me an idea. When the police came, we couldn't exactly say we were on a stakeout for the Grabber. I didn't want a lecture from the cops about how dangerous that was, and if my parents found out, they'd kill me themselves.

But they couldn't be too upset if we happened to see something suspicious while on our way to get pizza. Sansborough House of Pizza stayed open all night. We could say we were studying late and needed food. The way we went through pizza, it was a believable lie—and didn't reveal anything about ghosts or werewolves.

I veered back to Calvin and whispered my plan. He nodded and I ran to the alley where Simon waited.

"That stupid bloody girl," Simon said. "Thank God you stayed inside the car."

"I'm fine," I said.

His shoulders shuddered as tension left his body. Simon's relief was almost palpable. I wanted to reach out and reassure him with a hug, but other people needed my help right now...and his hands were busy holding the Grabber to the ground.

"I need to check on Sarah," I said.

He nodded, the skin tightening around his eyes. There were dark circles that hadn't been there before. Perhaps seeing Sarah Randall hadn't just been hard on Yuki. Simon had a lot of demons from his past. I made a mental note to talk to him about it later. I wanted to know all of his secrets, even the painful ones.

I moved to the rear of the van and lifted my hands, palm out.

"Sarah?" I asked. "My name is Emma and I'm here to help. There's an ambulance coming and the police are on the way. I'm sure your parents will be here soon too. Can I come in?"

Sarah lay on her side, shaking. Simon had managed to remove the bonds from her wrists. Her hands covered her face and the gag hung loosely below her chin. This girl had been through hell. I wasn't going to make that any worse by barging in on her. If she didn't want my help, I'd wait for the paramedics.

She moved her fingers and blinked against the harsh interior light of the van. I thought I saw recognition there and she nodded.

"Don't you...don't go to my school?" she asked.

"Yes, Wakefield High," I said, keeping my voice low. I was talking to her like I would a scared animal. "School's almost over. I can't wait for summer."

I started working on the rope that bound her ankles.

"Did he hurt you?" I asked.

My voice shook and I blinked tears from my eyes.

"No-o-o," she stuttered. "Not really. He liked to talk."

Oh my god, I really didn't want to know what that creep liked to talk about. I'm sure she didn't want to think about it either.

"Okay, your feet might tingle while the circulation comes back," I said, pulling off the last of the rope. "Can you sit up?"

I helped Sarah into a sitting position, moving closer when she swayed.

"Are you thirsty?" I asked.

"Yes," she said.

Sarah hiccupped and she started crying again. I pulled a bottle of water from my bag and handed it to her silently. Words dried up on my lips. What else could I possibly say to comfort her?

I leaned against the van while she cried, staying within sight. Simon continued to hold the Grabber to the ground, angling the man's face away from where I stood.

"Is the girl alright?" Simon asked.

"She will be, eventually," I said. I nodded at the man held beneath him. "At least she'll have the comfort of knowing that monster can't harm her anymore."

"No, love," he said. "This one won't be hurting anyone ever again."

Chapter 53
Calvin

Blue and red lights flashed across Yuki's pale face. An ambulance and a patrol car had arrived first and were soon joined by a second ambulance and a squad of local police vehicles. The first ambulance had taken Sarah Randall to the hospital. Yuki and I sat in the back of the second ambulance while in the street the moped driver assured a paramedic that he was fine.

Police were busy cordoning off this section of street, the alley, and the photography studio. We were now sitting in a crime scene.

A detective had taken our statement and gave me his card. The police seemed to believe our story of being students out on a late night pizza run. Simon had claimed that he was the one who spotted a man forcing a girl into the back of his van. Since he was the one kneeling on top of the body when the cops came, we let him take the credit.

The rest of us had received a reprimand for rushing out into oncoming traffic. Fortunately, Yuki and the cyclist hadn't received any major injuries. With a crime scene to attend to, and a notorious killer now in custody, the police had bigger fish to fry.

Yuki sucked in air through her teeth as a paramedic probed the cut on her head.

"You'll have a nasty bump, but it looks worse than it is," the paramedic said.

"Head wounds are always bleeders," a second paramedic said.

The first paramedic slapped a band-aid on the cut and clapped me on the back.

"You sure you two don't want to get checked out downtown?" he asked.

"No thank you," I said. "We'll be fine. We should be getting home."

"Tell your friend if she ever needs a job, give us a call," the second paramedic said, motioning toward where Emma stood. "She's got skills."

"Thanks, I'll tell her," I said.

I helped Yuki down from the ambulance and waved to Simon and Emma. Emma jingled her keys.

"Are we good to go?" she asked.

"Yes," I said. "Let's get out of here before the press catches wind of this. I don't want to end up on the news."

"And pass up my television debut?" Simon asked. He placed a hand on his chest. "Didn't you hear? I'm a hero."

Emma rolled her eyes.

"Let's go home," she said.

We got in the car and as the police lifted the tape for us to leave, Yuki's stomach growled.

"Hungry?" I asked.

"Well, you guys were all talking about pizza," she said.

I laughed, suddenly feeling giddy. We had done it. We caught the Grabber and rescued Sarah Randall. And, other than a few bumps and bruises, Yuki was fine.

"For once, I agree with you, love," Simon said. "I could eat a horse."

"You would, old man," she said.

"Oh my God, you two," Emma said. "Shut. Up."

Emma scowled at Yuki and Simon, but a smile tugged at the edge of her lips.

"I suppose we do have a few things to celebrate," I said. "Pizza party?"

"Pizza party!" Yuki and Simon shouted in unison.

Emma shook her head and changed lanes. It was time to celebrate.

Chapter 54
Yuki

The final week of school flew by in a whirlwind of exams and oral presentations. My painting received an A, helping me pass my art class, but the chances of passing some of my other subjects was iffy. With Emma and Cal's help, I studied every second that I wasn't in class. I still kept my fingers crossed, toes too.

I had finally decided what I wanted to do with my life after high school. But first I had to graduate. Flunking out and having to repeat the school year had joined the other nightmare scenarios that plagued my sleepless nights. Repeating senior year may not have been as life threatening as abduction by jocks or revenge by witches, but I was still terrified.

On Friday, the list of passing seniors was posted.

I passed.

I lifted my hands above my head and hooted, doing a victory dance. My skirts twirled as I spun all the way to my locker.

"Hey," I said, bumping into Emma.

"Are you alright?" she asked. "You don't look so good."

"I'm awesome," I said, grinning. "Just dizzy."

No more twirling for me. If I moved my head too fast, the hallway started to tilt, making my stomach go all twisty.

"I thought the paramedics said you were fine," she said. Emma narrowed her eyes and looked me over. "No concussion."

"Nope, I'm good," I said. I leaned in closer, like I knew the world's best secret. "Better than good. I'm totally freaking amazing."

"Do you mean what I think you mean?" Emma said.

"I passed," I said, bouncing on the toes of my boots. "You're looking at a graduate of Wakefield High."

"Squee!" we both squeeled.

We bumped knuckles and Emma pulled me into a hug. When Emma stepped back, she had a smug grin on her face.

"Well, I wasn't going to say anything until I knew for sure you were graduating," she said. "But...I got class valedictorian."

"That is so awesome," I said. "There are some scary smart people in our class. You rock!"

I started jumping up and down, and twirling. Didn't I decide not to do that again? I was instantly dizzy, but didn't care. I was too freaking happy.

"I did have a lot of competition," she said.

Emma tossed her head, flipping her hair over one shoulder. She was trying to look poised, like a true class leader, but a flush crept across her cheeks and I knew she was pleased with herself.

Me? I just kept dancing.

*****

It was the last day of school for seniors and the parking lot was filled with smiling faces. Speakers were blaring and someone had written "skool sux" with white chalk on the pavement. It was almost festive, but we didn't stick around to goggle at our classmate's antics.

We had a much more somber task to attend to.

Emma maneuvered her car past the chaos of the school parking lot and let out a sigh of relief. Classes were over. We just had one more assignment before we were official graduates. Tomorrow we would dress in ridiculously unflattering caps and gowns and accept our diplomas.

Walking across the stage in front of the entire student body? Yeah, I wasn't too thrilled about that. But if it meant freedom from Wakefield High, and the beginning of my dreams for the future, I'd do it. Plus, who cares if I have to wear a bright red muumuu? It's all about the accessories.

I was trying to decide if I wanted to go with a dramatic lace collar or spiky metal studs, when Emma cleared her throat. Her gaze flicked over at me, then back to the road.

"I'm really glad you're graduating with us," she said.

She sighed and ran her fingers through her hair.

"But?" I asked. When someone sighed like that, there is always a "but."

"I'm still worried about you," she said. "I know the past few months have been hard, ever since the football team stuck you in that closet. At first we weren't talking, and then I didn't want to pressure you, but...have you thought about your future?"

When she mentioned the football team, I felt like someone had slapped me in the face. I reached up to touch my cheek, but stopped. School was over. They couldn't hurt me anymore.

And Emma had a point. Until last week, I didn't have any plans for the future. Emma, Gordy, and Katie were all going off to college and Cal had his pack duties to attend to. But I hadn't even mentioned anything that I'd like to do once we graduated.

We had been so busy that I hadn't had a chance to talk to her about my plans. I guess too, I felt a bit superstitious about the whole thing. I was going to wait until I had something more concrete to show her, like a stack of paintings or a stall in the flea market with my name on it. *Oh well, no time like the present.*

"I'm going to pursue my art," I said. I looked down at my hands and picked at the flaking nail polish. I'd have to redo them before graduation tomorrow. "I may get a stall at the flea market, at least at first."

I felt foolish saying it out loud to Emma. It had sounded like such a great idea when I told Cal. But compared to Emma's plans, my dreams seemed childish. What was I thinking?

"Wow, that's a fantastic idea," she said. "Have you considered art school?"

"I don't know," I said. "Maybe, in the future. Right now I want to work on my paintings and make a go of it. I figure if I paint ghost auras, my art will be unique. And Cal said he'd help me get the stall set up."

"You are definitely one of a kind," she said teasingly. "Seriously though, I think it's a great idea. I'm even a little bit jealous."

"Jealous?" I asked. "No way."

"Really," she said. "I'm following my dream to go to veterinary school, but I can't follow my heart until I come home as a licensed vet. I know you're not crazy about Simon, but it's hard knowing we can't really be together until then. Part of me wishes I didn't have to go, that I could stay here with Simon. So if you open your art stall here in Wakefield, you have both Calvin and your art now. I have to wait."

"Oh," I said. "That sucks."

I hadn't really thought about it. I never questioned Emma leaving and going away to college. I'd miss her, but veterinary school was her dream. But if she really loved Simon, then he was part of her dreams now too. If I had to choose between something I loved and Calvin, I'd go crazy.

"Look on the bright side," she said. Emma let out a shaky laugh. "At least we have a future."

Emma pulled her car into a parking spot near the Wakefield Park front gates. Bouquets and wreaths of flowers rested against the stone pillars, where people had set up a memorial to Rose Peterson.

I felt suddenly guilty. Here I was worrying and complaining about our future plans when we were here to say goodbye to Rose, who didn't have a future anymore. She wouldn't be making plans for school or meeting a nice guy.

She was dead.

Chapter 55
Emma

The memorial to Rose Peterson had been growing all week, ever since our anonymous phone call to the police. Simon had bought a disposable cell phone and Calvin had made the call, letting some of his wolf come to the surface to disguise his voice. Then we watched the television and checked the Internet obsessively for news.

The day after our anonymous tip, the police held a press conference announcing the discovery of Rose Peterson's remains. Once the police completed their tests, her body would be released to her family and her soul could finally rest.

Yuki had been relieved that her responsibilities to Rose Peterson were over. But she still had one final task. It was time to say goodbye.

We stood looking at the flowers, stuffed animals, and candles. The people of Wakefield had felt the loss of this local teen deeply. At least with the Grabber behind bars, they wouldn't have to experience grief at his hands again. Thanks to our little group of friends, he would never be returning to Wakefield.

Calvin couldn't make it, but said he would keep Rose in his thoughts. I wondered what was so important that he'd miss this, but then a motorcycle engine purred and all thoughts of Calvin disappeared. Simon was here.

"Hello, Love," he said.

Simon walked to stand at my side, the crunch of gravel beneath his expensive boots the only sound. It was so peaceful here, the perfect place for a memorial.

We weren't at the site where Yuki originally found Rose. Police were still maintaining that area as a crime scene. But when the police reported her body being found in the park, people had shown up to remember her and honor her family's loss.

I swallowed the lump in my throat and reached for Simon's hand.

"Hey," I said.

Simon had thought to bring flowers. He squeezed my hand then knelt down to place the bouquet with the others. Reaching inside his jacket, he withdrew a candle. Brushing the ground, he set the votive there and, with a flick of his wrist, lit the candle with a lighter from his pocket. He bowed his head then stood, holding me close.

I looked over to where Yuki sat on the ground, her skirt pooled around her. Her lips were moving and she was smiling. She was saying goodbye.

I never really understood Yuki's connection to the ghosts that she helped. They plagued her with smells until she helped them with their final wishes, but in the end it seemed like they became friends. It gave me hope that Yuki would get her wish, that she could make it through Samhain without wearing Nera's amulet.

Yuki felt strongly about returning the amulet to its rightful owners. Her wishful belief was that the spirits of the dead whom she helped find peace would return to her side and aid her in her battle against the evil spirits who tried to harm her on Samhain. She hoped for an army of souls to keep her safe.

I looked at Yuki as she reached up and waved goodbye, a wistful smile on her lips as a tear rolled down her cheek.

More like an army of friends.

Chapter 56
Yuki

I woke up excited to breathe fresh, clean air. No more smelly ghosts. I had watched yesterday as Rose Peterson's glowing aura stepped into the light. She had finally found her peace.

I was ghost free. Even Jackson's vinegar scent was missing. I breathed in the smell of clean sheets and sighed. I smiled up at the ceiling, lazily counting the plastic constellations above my head. I could stay in bed all day. Then I remembered what day it was. *Son of a dung beetle.*

Today was graduation.

I sat up so quickly my head spun. Ugh. I threw the comforter back, jumped out of bed, and ran to my closet. A tomato red cap and gown hung on the back of the door. I'd have to put that ugly thing on over my clothes, but that didn't make choosing what to wear underneath any easier. Plus, I wouldn't be wearing the cap and gown all day.

What to wear, what to wear?

My parents had promised to take me and Cal out for afternoon tea in the garden view room at a local bed and breakfast. Tea, scones, and finger sandwiches, I couldn't wait. I was tempted to wear my "Dark Alice" costume for tea, but no. It was a rare occasion for both of my parents to take time off from work. I was going to dress nice.

Definitely the black, high necked, neo-Victorian dress.

I grabbed the dress, lace gloves, and a pair of button-up boots. Racing for the shower, I sent up a silent prayer; *please don't let me trip on stage.* At least my boots don't have laces. That should help even the odds.

I emerged an hour later in full dress and makeup. I strode to my full length mirror, skirts swishing. I'd chosen black and white striped stockings which showed above my boots where the skirts of my dress were cinched at the knee. The back of the dress flowed down to touch my boots about an inch above the heel. Oversleeping meant I didn't have time to paint my nails, but the lace gloves I wore covered the flecks of old black nail polish.

I was finally ready. I fist pumped the air above my head and stared back at my reflection.

"Time to graduate," I whispered.

*****

I sat beside my parents on an uncomfortable folding chair and fidgeted with my cap. I couldn't wait to throw the thing into the air, and be rid of it for good, but first I had to graduate.

The sun was rising high into the late morning sky and the heat was already unbearable. It felt like I'd been sitting in the heat for hours. Another drop of sweat trickled down my back. Why did they have to hold the ceremony outside? Not that I wanted to spend the day inside a smelly gym, but at least in there my makeup wouldn't run. I felt like I was melting.

"You look lovely, dear," Mom said.

"Thanks," I said

I caught motion to my right and perked up. Were we starting? My stomach filled with the flutter of vampire bats, but it was only Gordy waving. I waved back at Gordy and Katie who were taking their seats.

At least they wouldn't have to sit here as long. My parents had insisted on coming early. Looking at the program, I groaned. They were calling students in alphabetical order. With the name Stennings, I would be one of the last students to walk the stage. I just hoped that they called me Yuki.

A hand on my shoulder made me jump.

"Can I borrow Yuki for a moment, Mrs. Stennings?" Cal asked.

Ah, rescued by my knight in furry armor. My mom loved Cal, she'd totally say yes.

"Only for a few minutes, Calvin," she said. "They are preparing to begin."

"Be right back," I said, already rushing to leave.

Cal held out his hand and I climbed over the chair to exit the row of seats. I followed Cal to where Simon stood waiting beneath the shade of a tree.

"Simon has a graduation gift for you," Cal said.

Hell must have frozen over.

"Yes, I would have waited until after the ceremony, but Emma's parents have invited me to a family cookout," Simon said. He looked slightly ill. I wasn't sure if it was the thought of attending a cookout, meeting Emma's parents, or eating tofu dogs and veggie burgers. "Calvin told me about your decision to pursue painting as a career."

I nodded, wondering what kind of gift Simon would give me. A paint brush? A sketch pad? Instead he handed me a business card.

"If you're serious, and want to show your work in Boston some time, I know a guy with an art gallery," he said. Simon glanced at the card in my hand and a grin tugged at his lips. "Tell him Simon sent you."

Simon knew a guy with an art gallery? Of course he did, Simon had connections everywhere. Usually they were black market connections, but I doubted he was talking about a shady art gallery. Then again, this was Simon.

"Is this guy some kind of forger?" I asked.

"Not anymore," he said, shrugging.

Great, Simon was hooking me up with a former black market art dealer. But the guy had gone legit. I slid the card into my pocket. Who knows, maybe I'd have Emma look him up online and make sure he had a legitimate gallery.

"Thanks Simon," I said.

He drifted off to sit with Emma and I took a step back toward the rows of seats.

"Wait," Cal said. "I haven't given you my gift yet."

"I thought we were exchanging gifts later," I said. "I don't have yours with me."

"This is just part of your gift," he said.

Cal handed me an envelope. I could feel something hard inside and when I opened it, a key slid out onto my palm.

"The key to your heart?" I asked.

Cal leaned down and let his lips brush mine.

"You already have that," he said. "This is a key to the flea market. You are now the renter of stall number thirteen."

I jumped into his arms and he spun me around.

"Really?" I squealed.

"Really," he said. "We can go there after we have tea with your parents."

Cal really was the best boyfriend ever.

We rushed back to our seats and the ceremony began. With thoughts of my new art business racing through my head, time flew by. Before I knew it, they were calling Emma's name. She would be taking the stage again later for her valedictory speech. I was so freaking proud of her.

As soon as she stepped onto the stage a cheering and round of applause met my own. I looked around, seeing my friends smiling and clapping, but the cheering wasn't coming from the seats where students sat with their families. Did Emma bring her own fan club? It was possible. She'd volunteered at a lot of local businesses that helped animals.

But when Calvin took the stage the cheering began again. Cal hadn't volunteered with Emma, so who were the people cheering?

Soon, too soon, it was my turn. They called out for Vanessa Stennings. Of course they wouldn't get my name right. Oh well, I'm almost out of this place. *Goodbye, Wakefield High.*

I walked up onto the stage, careful not to trip as I took the stairs one at a time. I wanted to run. My lungs tightened and I started to see stars. But no, it wasn't stars. The golden glow was hovering over a family that stood arm in arm behind the rows of seats.

Rose Peterson had returned to witness one final victory.

I looked out past the now forgotten crowd to see Sarah Randall's smiling face. Sarah and her family cheered, laughing and clapping. They were cheering for me.

A blinked away tears and took a shuddering breath.

Senior year had been difficult—discovering that Cal was a werewolf, dealing with my emerging psychic powers, the car accident with Emma, and being bullied by jocks. Looking out at

Sarah's smiling face, I realized something important. My ability to smell spirits of the dead was not a curse, it was a gift. A weight lifted from my chest and for the first time in months, I could breathe again. My life may be difficult, but I wouldn't change it for the world.

I raised my hand and waved.

Author's Note

"My heart, always so strong in the past, was like the fishnet stockings that clung to my legs—torn, shredded, and full of gaping holes."
--Yuki, *Brush with Death*

The Spirit Guide series has been an emotional journey for me. These characters have been raised up, knocked down, and tormented, by bullies, ghosts, and their pasts, and yet they continue to pick up the pieces with a smile—until Brush with Death.

In the newest installment of the Spirit Guide series, there are chinks in the armor of these characters, and its beginning to show. You can't glue Humpty Dumpty back together over and over again and expect his smile to remain perfect. There will always be a twist to his lips here, a dark shadow beneath his eyes there. And that's what I wanted to show in Brush with Death. These characters are amazing and strong and true to themselves, but they are damaged.

Do they make mistakes? Yes. These are teens on the cusp of adulthood who are dealing with ghosts, bullies, creepy spirit guides, and (hopefully) high school graduation. Each character is under incredible pressure to make the right decisions about their future.

But it's hard to focus on tomorrow, if you may not survive the day.

I hope fans of the series will forgive me for the way I treated these beloved characters. I can assure you that I felt every moment of fear, guilt, and indecision as if it were my own. As one reviewer put it, "I hope you're ready to be torn apart and stitched back together again when you read it, because that's exactly what happened to me. Yuki was broken, Calvin was broken, Emma was broken, I was broken—but E.J. slammed us all back together and it wasn't awful, it was *good*." I will keep my fingers crossed that you find the overall experience good as well.

And if you are still with me, dear readers, in 2013 we have ghost pirates. Yes, GHOST PIRATES. I promise that The Pirate Curse will be fun indeed.

The Spirit Guide Series

She Smells the Dead
Yuki has a secret…she smells the dead.

"This series is like Nancy Drew meets the Winchester Brothers
from Supernatural."
-I'd So Rather Be Reading

Spirit Storm
Spirits of the Dead are coming…

"Part mystery, part adventure, part romance and all the things a
reader wants."
-Read For Your Future

Legend of Witchtrot Road
*Surviving agitated ghosts, irritated witches, angry werewolves, and
the horrors of high school has never been so hard.*

"I didn't think it possible to fall even more in love with this series
(and the characters, oh the amazingly swoon-worthy male
characters and the super snarky female characters), but after having
read this book, the third installment of this series, I found that it is
indeed possible."
-Avery's Book Nook

Brush with Death
Samhain was scary, but graduation is downright terrifying.

The Pirate Curse
*When Yuki starts smelling salt brine and seaweed, she finds her
summer vacation hijacked by pirates…the DEAD kind.
Will the ghost of Black Sam Bellamy, Prince of Pirates, lead Yuki
and her friends to treasure or terror?*
(Coming 2013)

The Ivy Ganger Series

Shadow Sight
*Welcome to Harborsmouth, where monsters walk the streets
unseen by humans...except those with second sight, like Ivy
Granger.*

"I recommend this book to anyone who enjoys sarcastic wit,
supernatural beings, a good mystery and one kick butt heroine."
-Paranormal Romance Guild

"I enjoyed it even more than my beloved Hollows series by Kim
Harrison."
-My Keeper Shelf

"If you're looking for a great urban fantasy read and love all things
fae and enjoy the October Daye series by Seanan McGuire, then I
highly recommend Shadow Sight as a great way to spend a few
hours inside the well spun fantastical world crafted by E.J.
Stevens"
-sfx555chick

"If you like the Kate Daniels magic series, you'll dig this one!!"
-Kris10karma

"Shadow Sight is a fun, quirky paranormal read that just leaves
you wanting more."
-The Bawdy Book Blog

Blood and Mistletoe: An Ivy Granger Novella
*Holidays are worse than a full moon for making people crazy. In
Harborsmouth, where many of the residents are undead vampires
or monstrous fae, the combination may prove deadly.*
(Coming November 2012)

Ghost Light
(Coming 2013)

E.J. Stevens is the author of the Spirit Guide young adult series and the bestselling Ivy Granger urban fantasy series. When E.J. isn't at her writing desk she enjoys dancing along seaside cliffs, singing in graveyards, and sleeping in faerie circles. E.J. currently resides in a magical forest on the coast of Maine where she finds daily inspiration for her writing.

You can learn more about E.J. by visiting
http://about.me/EJStevens